D1789497

THE JUDAS TRAIL

Unjustly accused of rape and savagely punished by the powerful Coulter family, Juan Laredo enlists the support of the notorious outlaw Delaney to wreak revenge on the Coulters. They in turn look to bounty-hunter Cade Forster to track down Laredo and his gang. Cade soon uncovers a plot of treachery and greed, bringing about the downfall of the Coulters.

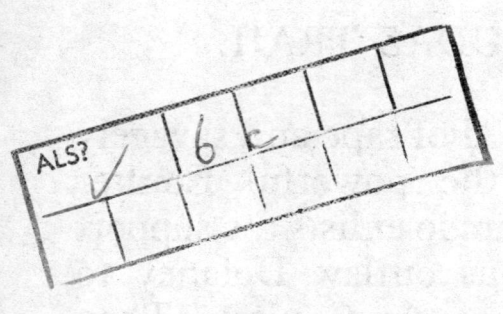

E. G. STOKOE

THE
JUDAS TRAIL

Complete and Unabridged

CHESHIRE
LIBRARIES
15 APR 1991
4178

LINFORD
Leicester

First published in Great Britain in 1988 by
Robert Hale Limited
London

First Linford Edition
published April 1991
by arrangement with
Robert Hale Limited, London

Copyright © 1988 by E. G. Stokoe
All rights reserved

British Library CIP Data

Stokoe, E. G. (Edward George) *1919* –
The Judas Trail.—Large print ed.—
Linford western library
I. Title
813.54 [F]

ISBN 0–7089–7012–5

Published by
F. A. Thorpe (Publishing) Ltd.
Anstey, Leicestershire
Set by Words & Graphics Ltd.
Anstey, Leicestershire
Printed and bound in Great Britain by
T. J. Press (Padstow) Ltd., Padstow, Cornwall

For
Keith and Malcolm

The Beginning ^A

THEY pounced on Laredo in the dead of night, pistol-whipped him across the head and dragged him from the ranch-house to a buckboard where he was lashed and bound to one of the high standing wheels. There the shirt was torn from his back and he was whipped mercilessly until even his fierce Mexican pride could stand no more. His shrieks brought satisfaction to all but one of the tiny knot of witnesses. Kit Coulter was uneasy, but made no effort to stay the brawny arm of his brother Ben from wielding the whip.

The punishment over, the ranch foreman stepped forward and slashed at the ropes binding Laredo. Caught before he slumped to the ground, he was slung into the back of the buckboard like a carcase of beef. Tears of pain and humiliation stung his eyes as he

1

lay groaning on the bare boards. The party scrambled aboard, out snaked Ben's rawhide whip over the necks of the mounts and the buckboard trundled out of the ranch and into the plain.

At length the rolling grassland gave way to stony irregular ground and Laredo knew they had reached the badlands where lonely buttes stood eternal sentry and giant cacti sheltered snake and lizard.

The buckboard came to a halt and he was hauled from its depths and taken to a soft patch of earth where he was staked out like some animal pelt. His tormentors worked silently and expertly and when they had finished piled up again into the buckboard and drove off into the night.

Laredo twisted and writhed until both wrists were bleeding but there was no escaping the cruel ropes. He slumped in his bonds, feeling a moving sensation on his raw back. Exploring insects were beginning to add to his torture. By sundown tomorrow his eyeballs would be seared by the scorching sun and scaly-headed buzzards moving in on him with their hideous raucous croaking. He strained in his bonds once more, arched his agonised back and screamed at the scudding moon, "Coulters, God rot every one of you!"

A repulsive fat-tailed lizard stirred uneasily in a nearby crevice, sensed that there was no danger, and went back to sleep.

Part One

1

Gun For Hire

A

IN a territory renowned for its violence the cattle town of Durward was supreme. Quiet as the surrounding plain by day, it was a roaring bedlam by night with drunken brawls, shootings, knifings and clubbings. It never asked a man his name but what he would like to be called. It had half a dozen brothels and as many dance-halls, fourteen saloons and five gambling houses, and its inhabitants were a good cross-section of those who made up the West in the Seventies: plainsmen, medicine drummers, cowhands, peons, mule freighters and prostitutes. Arkansas Amy put over a rip-roaring act each night on the stage of the 'Silver Dollar' and an even better one in an upstairs room. Scar-faced Lil at the 'Ace Saloon' was a more talented performer, but not as entertaining after her show, whilst Oklahoma Kathie at the 'Western Star' outstripped both Amy and Lil in every sense of the word.

It was late in the afternoon when Cade Forster reached town. He rode his bay at a trail-gait down its wagon-rutted main street until he came to Saul Stein's Bank, noting with satisfaction that a two-storeyed saloon stood opposite — the 'Silver Dollar'. There were few people around at this time of day, a knot of gossiping women, a couple of homesteaders loading a big Missouri mule and a drunken vaquero serenading himself with a battered guitar on the high-boarded sidewalk.

Crossing the road, he reined in by the saloon and stiffly dismounted. It had been a long, hard ride. He let the bay have his fill at the trough, tied him to the hitching-rail then withdrew his Winchester from its dusky scabbard. Holding the rifle in the crook of his arm, he pushed open the batwings and went into the saloon. It was almost empty. Some peons with palm-leaf sombreros shading their dusky faces sat huddled around a bottle in one corner, chatting in low voices so as not to disturb the concentration of the half-dozen cowpokes in the middle of the room playing poker. Each player had a fistful of cards and a shot of rye at their elbows. None of them spoke but studied the fan of cards in their hands as though their very lives depended on them. Maybe they did, thought Cade, making his way over to the bar. Slung very low and fixed to a heavy belt were his twin quick-draw holsters, the notched handles of his shooting-irons clearly visible against their leather background.

"Got a room?" asked Cade.

Charlie, the bar-keep, looked up from polishing a glass. When he took in the stranger the sarcastic quip died on his lips. This was no cowpokin' buckaroo. He had the hard-boned face of the desert-rider.

"Sure," replied Charlie, dislodging an

irritating fly from his squidgy nose. "Number thirteen okay?"

"Overlooks the bank?"

Curiosity showed in the bar-keep's eyes but he fought against it. "Sure does," he said with a respect that was alien to him. "Plumb opposite."

"I'll take it."

Cade fished in the pocket of his bullhide vest and drew out a tiny sack of gold-dust tied with twine. He tossed it on to the mahogany and it landed with a dull, inviting plop. "That should take care of things for awhile. Have a bottle sent up to my room."

Cade moved towards the stairway then turned. "Short hombre, scar down his left cheek, answers to the name of Mitch — has he shown up in town?"

Charlie shook his head regretfully. "Don't know the guy."

Cade gave the bar-keep a lingering look then continued towards the stairs.

Charlie, greedily clutching the tiny sack, blew out his cheeks in relief. He was glad to see the back of the tall, hard-eyed stranger and didn't envy Mitch, whoever he was. If Mitch could get away from this gunfighter he would have to run faster than a bullet.

The room was small, adequate and astonishingly clean. There was even a bunch of freshly-cut flowers in the vase on the plain deal dressing-table. Some woman's touch no doubt.

Cade threw his battered sombrero on the bed and crossing over to the open window set down his Winchester.

He looked down at the bank opposite. On one side of it stood an ornate building which looked like a bordello and on the other a funeral parlour with a newly-painted sign above the door — 'The Last Round Up'. A ghost of a smile hovered round Cade's lips. There was still little activity in the street below, the women having dispersed to seek shelter from the scorching sun. The heat sucked like an octopus with a thousand tentacles.

Cade turned back into the room, built himself a smoke, and stretched his length along the bed. He lay blowing smoke-rings at the timbered ceiling, yawning occasionally. He was weary, dusty, but knew that the end of the trail was in sight. The bar-keep had reason to feel in awe of Cade Forster, whose toughness was ingrained and deep. Nursed in the savage frontier ways, he knew the stars and the winds and all the quaint customs of the Indian nations, Apache, Cherokee, Hopi and even the Iroquois way up north.

A discreet knock at the door cut across his train of thought. "Come in," he sang out, propping himself up on his elbows.

It was a girl with a tray bearing a bottle and a glass. She was about eighteen, olive-skinned and raven-haired. In her off-shoulder blouse and flared skirt she looked part, if not all, Mexican. She set down the tray on a small table by the bed and looked down at Cade. "Pour you a drink, senor?"

"Later."

She stood back, looking at him uncertainly.

"Well?" he asked.

Colour crept into her cheeks. "Do you want me now — or later?"

So the tiny sack of gold-dust bought more than booze and a bed, thought Cade. "What's your name?"

"Maria, senor."

"Uhuh — and how long have you worked here, Maria?"

"Five, maybe six months."

His eyes softened. "You cut a nice vase of flowers, Maria — got any more talents? Sing? Dance maybe?"

The girl suppressed the anger she felt rising within. She liked this tall stranger with the corn-coloured hair but resented the implication of his questions. She could neither sing nor dance but she was damned if she was going to join the bevy of hard-faced women employed by Jake La Rue. Bad enough cleaning rooms of the 'Silver Dollar' with its occasional sexual demands but a girl without kinfolk had to do something to earn a living.

"No," she answered shortly, but as

though excusing herself. "I once worked at the Two Bark, biggest spread in the territory. I was a personal servant to Miss Lucinda but something happened and I had to leave."

"Had to leave," echoed Cade. "Eh well, you're a lovely girl, Maria, but I won't be wanting you now or ever. Thanks for bringing the drink." The smile in his eyes was as attractive as an early sunrise.

Confused, relief flooding her cheeks, Maria just nodded and made towards the door. Hand on the knob, she turned and murmured almost apologetically "If there's anything else you want, senor?"

Cade shook his head and she left, wondering what excuse she could find to revisit the room.

He lay back on the bed, moodily surveying the bottle and glass until the clip-clop of hooves through the open window shot him to his feet. Dousing the quirly, he crossed swiftly to the open window, hand closing over the Winchester. In the street below five riders armed to the teeth were rapidly dismounting outside Stein's Bank.

Two of the riders rushed to grab the reins of all the horses whilst the other three, Colts at the ready, were heading for the bank.

From his vantage perch in the window Cade took aim.

His finger squeezed lovingly round the trigger and the first shot rang out, shattering the stillness of the afternoon air and sending skywards flocks of birds in raucous protest.

The outlaw nearest to the bank door pitched forward on to his face as though pole-axed and the others spun round in amazement, wondering who had fired.

Cade did not hesitate. In rapid succession shots went winging their way with unerring aim and he smiled grimly as each outlaw in turn reeled drunkenly, staining either sidewalk or roadway a bright crimson. All hell broke loose in the street. People came pouring open-mouthed out of doorways but drew back swiftly to avoid the outlaws' horses.

Freed from lifeless hands, they were careering along the street, their eyes rolling in fright.

Cade left the saloon in icy calm, the rifle in the crook of his arm still smoking. He went up to the carnage and viewed it with distaste but satisfaction. All five, dead as doornails.

He turned over one of the twitching bodies with the toe of his riding-boot. The man's left cheek was badly scarred and there was a neat hole in the centre of his forehead. Another quest over, thought Cade; weeks of careful tracking had paid off.

He looked across at the white-faced man standing in the entrance of the bank. He was staring at Cade in disbelief. "Do you own this bank?" asked Cade.

"Y-yes," quavered Saul Stein, shaken by the lightning execution and the bank's narrow escape.

Cade nodded towards the next-door funeral parlour. "Sun's powerful strong so you'd best get these men planted pronto." He tapped the body at his feet.

16

"This here is Joe Mitchell, wanted down San Ferento way for more crimes than a burro's got hairs. Your bank has had a lucky escape, Mr Stein. Before you plant this lot I'd be obliged if you would sign me an affidavit to say that I gunned down Mitchell. That way I can collect. The rest are no-accounts, only Mitch matters. The name's Forster — Cade Forster."

"I surely will, Mr Forster, I surely will. You'll have the document within the hour . . . " Words failed him. A bounty hunter b'God, and wouldn't he be with such fancy shooting. He stared in admiration as Cade walked back to the saloon.

The street was agog with excitement and there was admiration in more than the bank manager's eyes. Jess Coulter, youngest of the three Coulter brothers, had leapt from Nell James' bed at the sound of Cade's first shot and from the upstairs window of the bordello had witnessed the execution. To Nell's frustration and annoyance, Jess was down in the street in a flash, greedy for news.

Maria too had seen the killings, and though appalled by the slaughter was thrilled to the marrow of her bones.

Reaching his room, Cade took his fill of rye then stretched out again on the bed. He was soon asleep, the first good one in several weeks.

Commotion still reigned in the street. Stein had arranged with Jasper Simpson, owner of the funeral parlour, to have the outlaws buried at the bank's expense, and a spotty-faced youth, who worked for Jasper, had laid the bodies side by side after swilling down the sidewalk. Four were recognised and the cry went up 'the Galton brothers', quickening the interest of the folk flocking round. No one seemed to know the one with the scarred face. The Galtons, however, once had a reputation for skulduggery in the area, until they had moved to pastures new.

Nell James, clambered into her clothes and with a new girl at her side — Emma Carson — , hurried after Jess but was too late. He had gone. The pair joined the throng viewing the bodies.

"Ugh!" exclaimed Nell, wrinkling her nose.

Emma murmured, "The one with the scar reminds me of someone."

"The Devil?" grunted Nell.

"That's who I had in mind," replied Emma with a shudder then, under her breath, "Only he calls himself Delaney."

2

ADAM COULTER, the most successful and the most hated of all the cattle barons in the territory, sat with mounting fury in his high-backed chair overlooking the ranch patio. Only his injured leg, gored by a snake-startled steer some six years ago, prevented him from leaping to his feet and pacing the room.

Laredo — that no-account peon. How dare he threaten the peace and stability of the Two Bar X, the ranch he had forged with his own two hands more years ago than he cared to remember. Hundreds of acres of rolling grassland stocked with both long and shorthorns, the finest spread in the County.

As a junior member of John Durward's pioneering wagon-train — the same who had given his name to the town — Adam had laid claim to the virgin land and over the years had developed it to the envy it was today. During those years he had defended it against dispossessed Mexicans, rustlers and bands of marauding Apaches. In one such foray with Indians his wife Annabel had succumbed to an arrow dipped in rotted deer liver, leaving him to fend for their four children — Ben, the twins Kit and Lucinda, and Jess. Obsession with the ranch, which he had ruled with a rod of iron, had subdued all interest in the children, leaving him withdrawn, embittered and lonely. Only Martha, daughter of a long-dead friend and married to Ben, had any influence over him, probably because she alone tended to his needs.

Laredo. At first he had not believed that the Mexican had returned to avenge himself, but why had Coulter gold been stolen from the bank in San José? Why had Coulter cattle been rustled in the past month? And, more important, why had attempts been made on the lives of both Ben and Kit? A slug had hit Ben's saddle-horn during a cattle drive; an inch higher and it would have lodged in his belly. Kit's escape from a viciously thrown knife in the town had been equally miraculous.

Laredo was behind everything and it raised several questions.

How had the Mexican escaped the stake-out, where had he found the dinero to finance a band of outlaws, and most of all what was he, Adam Coulter, going to do about it. The veins in his temples moved like nests of disturbed worms. Involuntarily he glanced down at his mutilated hand. Many years ago needle-sharp fangs of a rocksnake had poured venom into his thumb and in a flash he had grabbed his hunting-knife and had slashed off the offending digit. That's what he would like to do to this goddam Mexican, hack off his masculinity as he had done to his forefathers who had tried to wrest the Two Bar X from him. If only he could get out of this chair . . .

Hearing the clatter of hooves he looked up sharply and saw Jess dismounting in the patio. Empty-headed numbskull, thought Adam, whoring the afternoon away in Scar-faced Lil's parlour when there was work to be done about the ranch. Ben had little business sense but leastways he was a worker. Kit was shrewd, but he could make nothing of him. Just looked back at you with those mocking eyes, saying nothing to offend but the merest hint of insolence in the set of his mouth. Damn them all: not one of them was half the man he was in his day.

Ignoring the baleful glare from the window Jess stalked into the house looking for Ben. He found him in the kitchen oiling his guns.

"Just left Durward and guess what," said Jess, knuckling sweat from his eyes. "A raid on Stein's Bank."

Ben glanced up.

"Five of 'em but they didn't get a goddam thing. Shot down before they even made the front door. Saw it with my own eyes. The whole town's talking about it. There was this guy in an upstairs window in the 'Silver Dollar' picking them off like wood pigeons. Cool as you like. All five were buzzard meat before they got to the door. Spoke to Saul Stein afterwards and guess what?" Enthusiasm bubbled in Jess's voice. "The killer was a bounty hunter, name of Cade Forster. Get the swing of it, Ben? A bounty hunter."

Ben carefully set down his guns on the table and began wiping his hands with the oily rag. "Laredo?"

Jess smacked the table with glee. "Laredo. Hire this Forster guy and we'll soon be rid of the greaseball. Even the Old Man will go for that, eh Ben?"

The more Ben thought about the idea the more it appealed to him. Bounty hunters were a rare, professional breed, highly-skilled and accountable only to themselves.

"Have you talked to Forster?"

"No," replied Jess, reaching for the apple-juice to quench his thirst.

"So you don't know when he's leaving town?"

"Asked Charlie but he didn't know.

Neither did Maria. After the killing the guy just locked himself in his room. Maria said he looked bushed so maybe he's pounding the pillow till sun-up."

"Maria okay?" Ben sounded anxious.

Jess shook his head impatiently. "Quit worrying, Ben; the girl hasn't talked and won't ever. She wouldn't dare. Well, do we see him or not?" Jess nodded towards Adam's room.

Ben left off rubbing his unshaven chin and got to his feet. He would see Adam but whatever the old man said he was determined to seek out this Cade Forster. That slug in the saddle had frightened him more than he cared to admit and if this bounty hunter could be hired the threat to the Two Bar X might quickly be resolved.

Wisely Ben conferred with his wife before approaching the rancher. Martha was wholly supportive and together they went to see Adam who sat scowling in his chair, clutching his stick. He listened in silence to Ben's suggestion and although he saw merit in the idea could not resist taunting him with a flow of sarcasm. Three brothers — couldn't just one of them risk his hide to settle scores with this Mexican? And how had he escaped in the first place? God, if it wasn't for this damned leg he would saddle up here and now and shoot the daylights out of the greaseball. It was all nonsense of course, and the rancher knew it. Where to begin tracking down Laredo and his band and how much time could be spared with so big a spread to manage? Alarmed by the suffusion of dark anger gathering in Ben's bull neck, Martha in her quiet confident way, steered the talk into calmer waters, and at length Adam gave way, which he had intended to do from the outset. "Okay," he growled. "Get this gunslinger Forster, whatever the cost."

As Ben left the room he thought he heard a quiet chuckle, cut short by Martha's sharp reprimand. The old bastard had had his quota of baiting for the day and was satisfied.

Ben called for his horse, a beautifully proportioned stallion with four white fetlocks, and a peon trotted up with it. Ben swung himself up into the saddle in a single easy movement, bit deeply with the rowels, and the horse bounded off towards the plain with a protesting snort. The glare of the afternoon had given way to the cool of the evening and high in the sky feathery clouds drifted. They were the 'mares' tails' which spoke of approaching rain. As these great tongues of flame grew yet brighter with the lowering sun the blue around them drained away until the sky was as calm as a summer sea.

Leaving the plain, Ben galloped into the long, low, wooded valley which led to the town.

Cut with the sharpness of a cameo against the sky, the horseman sat quite still watching the valley below. Across the pommel of his saddle and strikingly foreshortened lay his rifle which he held in his right hand. In his left he loosely held the reins.

Suddenly he stiffened. He had

recognised the rider and his mount going hell-for-leather through the valley. His rifle was up in a flash and he took careful aim.

Ben glanced to his left, saw the menacing figure, but was too late. The shot struck him in the heart, throwing him violently along the spine of his animal and over its rump. The stallion reared, whinnied and went racing off along the valley.

The killer manoeuvred his roan down the rocky hillside and rode up to view the crumpled body. Viciously he pumped more slugs into the corpse, spat and rode on.

Jed Harker straightened his aching back, wiped his brow, and glanced out of his forge. A riderless stallion was meandering down the street, reins trailing in the dust. Jed's eyes widened. There was no mistaking Ben Coulter's horse, he would know it anywhere, but where was Ben?

Jed raised the alarm and some time later a party of searchers found Ben's lead-filled body lying near a clump of juniper bush.

News of his death spread like a prairie fire, electrifying the town and the outlying ranches.

Who had dared to shoot down the heir to the Two Bar X — and why?

3

"NAME'S Jess Coulter, Mr Forster, that was my brother Ben who was gunned down last night. He was on his way to see you when he was killed. My father has sent me instead. Adam Coulter. Maybe you've heard of him. Owns the Two Bar X. We — we need your help, Mr Forster."

Cade nodded towards the back room of the saloon. "We'll talk in there. Charlie! A bottle in the backroom."

"Comin' right up, Mr Forster."

The pair sat facing each other across a small table. Rain was beating a tattoo on the small window. Charlie came in with a bottle of rye, eyed Jess with curiosity, and withdrew. Cade poured a drink for Jess and the youth tossed it back in one. Some colour crept into his cheeks. He looked as though he hadn't slept overnight.

"Your father wants me to bring in Ben's killer."

"Yes. He'll pay well."

"Why has he sent you?"

"Adam's crippled. A longhorn took him in the leg years ago. Hardly leaves his room. Adam's mean, Mr Forster, but it's not only him I'm worried about. There's my sister Lucinda and my other brother Kit. Last fall some Mexican by the name of Laredo got into the ranch-house during the night and attacked my sister in her bedroom. Raped her. God knows how he got in. Ben and Kit caught him, and on Adam's orders we took out the greaseball and flogged him. No one saw it 'cept maybe Maria, the girl who works here. She was my sister's servant. We don't want anyone in town to know about this; my sister's a mighty proud woman."

"She'd never seen this Mexican before?"

"No. None of us had. But he must have seen Lucinda at some time. We don't know how he got into the house but reckon it must have been through

31

the wood at the back. That's how Adam had the house built, timber at the back in case of siege. One time hostiles were always attacking and the wood was an escape route."

"How was he caught, Jess?"

"Kit heard scuffling in Lucinda's room, got hold of Ben and they burst in. Pistol-whipped the polecat. Adam was told about it and, like I say, on his orders Laredo was taken out and flogged. I was there and so was Slim Jackson, the ranch foreman."

Cade lit a quirly and studied the glowing end with a cool detachment. "So no one but family and the foreman knew anything about all this? None of the vaqueros?"

"No — Lucinda's prouder than a peacock. If the cowhands got to hear about it she'd be the laughing-stock of the spread. God knows what she would do to herself. 'Sides, they're all peons, they'd all be on the side of Laredo. Only Maria knew what happened and maybe even saw the flogging, but we got rid of her next morning with orders to keep her trap shut."

"What happened after the flogging?" asked Cade, eyeing Jess closely.

"Turned him loose," the other replied glumly.

Cade's eyes widened a little.

"Once knew a pony-soldier who tormented a rattler then turned him loose into the bush. Next morning he and three others were crow-bait. Your father's not so mean as you make him out to be."

Jess looked uncomfortable and reached for the bottle. "Yeh," he said a shade too quickly. "We should have strung the greaseball up."

"What does he look like?"

"Tall for a Mexican, good-looking. When we lashed him to the buckboard I noticed one of his fingers was missing."

"What makes you all so goddam sure it was Laredo who gunned down your brother?"

"Trouble started about two weeks ago. First there was the bank hold-up in San

José when a whole heap of Coulter gold was stolen, then Two Bar X cattle began to be rustled. When Ben was shot at and Kit almost knifed we were certainsure that it was the Mex. He must have rounded up others to help him. Ben and me wanted to go after him and his gang but Adam, for all his talk, was against it and wouldn't listen. Reckoned there was too much to be done about the spread and couldn't spare us. Locating Laredo would be like looking for a needle in a haystack he figured, and we would need a posse. No use taking our vaqueros; they would have soon helped Laredo. Kit sided with the old man, so we did nothing. And now Ben's dead. We need help Mr Forster."

Cade doused the butt of his smoke and got to his feet. "I'll want to know a deal more about this business, Jess, so tell your father to expect me around noon. I've got me some business in town to attend to first." His voice softened. "Best get some shut-eye, son. You look plumb tuckered out."

The Two Bar X lay in the snake bend of

a river amid a wide expanse of plain. To the south-west were the badlands which preceded the mighty range known as the Sierras del Oro, its peaks forever lost in a milk-white haze. The ranchhouse, built of stout pine, was both picturesque and impressive, and was backgrounded by a copse of tall cottonwoods. The timber walls of the house were scarred in many places by bullet, lance and arrow, bearing testimony to the assaults of former years. Some distance from the house were the bunkhouses which housed the swarthy Mexican vaqueros.

When Cade arrived at the ranch he found no sign of mourning. It was a hive of activity despite the noonday sun. Several bands of peons sweated as they repaired sections of broken fencing whilst another group, astride dumpy-short-legged cowponies, were rounding up cattle for the branding.

A leather-garbed figure detached itself from this group and cantered over to him. Cade reined in and held his bay in check.

"Cade Forster?" the other asked, and Cade nodded. "Kit Coulter. Welcome to the Two Bar X. The boss is expecting you. Jess has told us all about you. Thought we could handle this business our own way but it's gone too far. Like Jess says, we need help."

Again Cade nodded, overtly appraising the other. Far more handsome than Jess, he looked as though he could charm a bird off a tree. Mocking blue eyes and clean-cut features. Lucinda's twin. The heat didn't seem to be getting to him, cool as a cucumber. Nonetheless Cade's silence was disconcerting, especially when allied to his searching gaze. Kit didn't like being weighed up but controlled his resentment as he went on affably, "I'll ride with you to the ranch-house. Jess warn you about the Boss? He's got a mighty sharp tongue so you've got to keep yourself in check."

Cade took up the reins again and Kit fell in alongside. Together they rode towards the house. "Some spread," observed Cade, breaking his silence.

"Huh? Yeh, yeh . . . none like it in the territory," enthused Kit. "A man would have to ride a powerful long way to see another like it. And see that house? All pine and much of the furniture brought in from the east. One time it was always being raided by either Indians or greaseballs, even when I was a kid, but I reckon those days are gone. Well, I don't think you'll see any more of Jess today and my sister will be taking siesta but Martha will be up and about. She's Ben's wife . . . widow . . . Taking it well, is Martha. Looks after the Boss, y'know. Nobody else would. Got a mighty sharp tongue."

As the pair dismounted outside the house a peon emerged from the shade of a tree to tether the reins to a hitching-rail. Kit sauntered up to the open door and Cade followed.

Martha had seen them from the window and went to meet them. Cade saw that her eyes were red from weeping.

"Martha, this is Cade Forster," Kit said gravely.

She looked up at Cade. He was taller even than Kit. He touched the brim of his hat with old-world courtesy and murmured, "Pleased to make your acquaintance, ma'am."

Martha merely nodded and said, "Mr Coulter's waiting for you. Come in."

Stepping into the cool, shady interior of the ranch-house, Cade thought that she must have been a handsome woman in her day but living in this household had taken toll. What kind of man had Ben Coulter been that such a once pretty woman should looked so cowed. Had he been solely to blame or had the formidable rancher had a hand in it. When he got back to the 'Silver Dollar' he would speak to Maria about this and other things.

Kit left them with a sympathetic grin and Martha showed him to Adam Coulter's room.

Sitting in his high-backed chair facing him, Cade's first impression of Adam Coulter was one of sheer frustrated

38

power, like some hidden spring, within his broad frame. Inactivity through his injury had obviously bitten deeply into his soul, aggravating immeasurably his basic sardonic disposition. He had a mane of snow-white hair swept back from his forehead and a thin aristocratic nose. Latent cruelty lurked in the deep lines bracketing his thin-lipped mouth. He had large capable hands which kept clasping the handle of his stick. Cade saw that one of his hands had been savagely mutilated.

"My son Jess speaks highly of you, Mr Forster, although that is no compliment," said Adam in his dry, rasping voice. "All his brains are in his ass, only good for whoring. Still, even he can recognise a gunfighter when he sees one. And that's what we need right now, a gunfighter to bring in this greaseball, dead or alive. How much are you asking, Mr Forster?" The rancher flexed his mouth into the semblance of a smile, a disconcerting habit which was lost on Cade.

Cade remained silent, returning the

rancher's penetrating stare with cool appraisal.

"What's the matter?" snapped Adam. "Heat gotten to you? I asked how much, boy."

"Mr Coulter," said Cade easily, getting to his feet. "The last hombre that called me boy I used his hide for moccasins for some Mexican kids down San Ferento way. Maybe you'd like to know why I've ridden out here. I wanted to see the spread. It's the best I've seen and a man is to be complimented on such an achievement. Then I wanted to talk to the man who made it, a man who calls Mexicans greaseballs but lets one of them off with a flogging after he's raped his daughter."

Lines of caution began fanning out from the rancher's eyes. This was no saddle-tramp out to make a buck for collecting bad guys' scalps. He was a professional.

"Sit down, Mr Forster, sit down: sure I let him off with a flogging. Who'd think a goddam peon would have the gall to show up here again?"

"Some can be mighty proud. Once they ruled this territory."

"Greaseballs. Bandits at heart. I employ a hell of a lot of them on this spread. If they weren't working here, what do you think they'd be doing? Raising hell from here to the Sierras. Give me an Apache or a Mescalero any day. A man knows where he stands with them but a goddam Mex has more twists to him than a goddam sidewinder. Sure, I should have strung the bandit up, and we wouldn't be in the fix we are today. So how much are you asking to bring him in? Payment in gold-dust."

Cade remained standing.

"Once knew a pony-soldier who went on furlough and caught his wife with another man. He killed the guy, but never did get to know his name."

"And what's that supposed to mean, Mr Forster?"

"Think about it, Mr Coulter. Some Mexican none of you have seen before creeps in out of those woods and is

41

caught raping your daughter. How come you all know his name is Laredo? Have a nice long parley with him before he was flogged? No, Mr Coulter; this story's as crooked as a burro's hind leg. Good-day to you."

Cade rammed on his sombrero with the badly-scuffed brim and made for the door. He turned and looked at the rancher. "Maybe I will go after Laredo. I'd sure like to hear what he has to say."

"Killed my son, hasn't he?" snarled Adam, struggling to his feet.

"What would you do to an hombre that's taken a rawhide whip to your back?"

"Mexican lover," hissed Adam.

Hearing Cade leave, Kit hurried from the ranch-house.

"All okay?"

Cade casually untied his mount and swung himself up into the saddle. "Best talk to your father. Reckon he'll have some things to say to you." He nodded significantly towards the house. "Hope I

42

haven't disturbed your sister's siesta."

The flurry of movement behind Kit had not been lost on Cade. Kit flushed and looked uncomfortable.

Cade smiled tightly, lightly spurred the bay and, with a murmur of *"hasta luego"*, rode off.

Kit stood watching him until a weary voice called out:

"Mr Coulter wants to see you, Kit."

The ever-present, ever faithful Martha.

Riding through herds of longhorn cattle, tough, wiry creatures capable of moving a thousand miles without exhaustion, Cade reached the southern boundary of the ranch where a group of vaqueros were erecting barbed wire fencing. One of them left the group and flagged him down.

"Mr Forster?"

Not a peon, but his face so tanned he could easily have been taken for one.

"I'm Cade Forster."

"Slim Jackson, ranch foreman. Heard tell Mr Coulter's hiring you to round up this pesky Laredo."

"Aiming to. What do you know about him?"

"Goddam trouble-maker. If'n he shows up around here I'm good and ready for him." He patted his sideguns and shot tobacco-juice at a clump of grass.

"Bunk in the ranch-house, Slim?"

"Me? Naw. Got me the shack right next to it."

"So the night Laredo was taken the Coulters called for you?"

"Sure did, and Mr Ben, God rest his soul, sure taught him one hell of a lesson."

"Then let him go?"

Slim squinted his eyes against the glare of the sun and showed the same discomfort Jess and Adam had done.

"Shore hope you catch the polecat," he mumbled, and shuffled off back to the group watching with overt curiosity.

When Cade got back from the Two Bar X Maria was waiting for him in his room. Her eyes were bright with unshed tears. She looked at him accusingly and said in a low voice, "Hired you, haven't they? Want you to bring in Juan Laredo? Por Dios! there's nothing their money cannot buy."

Cade unbuckled his holster-belt and threw it on the bed. "Sit down, Maria," he said, motioning her to a chair. "Now tell me what you know about all this business. Why are you so all-fired het up about bringing in this Mexican, an hombre who rapes a girl then guns down her brother?"

Maria's eyes flew open.

"Rape?" she gasped. "Rape? Is that what they told you? Juan never raped anyone in his life. Never." Her words came gushing out in a torrent of passion, part Spanish. "He had been meeting Lucinda for weeks before the night they were caught. I should know, senor — I used to help them. At first they met in the woods and I used to keep watch, then later in the ranch-house. I pleaded with Miss Lucinda not to bring him into the house but she just laughed. He used to come through the wood at the back and I would shine a light and let him in. All the time he was in the house I was scared. Old Adam hates Mexicans and I knew what would happen if Juan was caught. Hates Mexicans though he uses them for labour, mean devil."

Cade looked thoughtful. "So it was Lucinda who invited Laredo into the house."

"I begged her not to, begged her, but she insisted."

"How many times did he come?"

"Only three, and on the third time he was caught. How, I don't know. Ben and Kit Coulter just burst into the room and grabbed him. I heard them but didn't see them. I was in a small room near Miss Lucinda's room. But I did see Juan dragged to a buckboard and whipped. The moon was up that night. After they whipped him they took him out to the badlands and staked him out. I knew they would. That's what Adam Coulter does to all who cross him."

"Staked out!" Cade whistled softly. No

wonder they had all been so goddam shifty. No death more cruel than a stake-out.

"Yes — just the way the Apaches do. Worse than Indians, the Coulters; but they don't want it known. I was kicked off the ranch the next morning and warned to keep my mouth shut or they'd kill me. Haven't told a soul until now. I'm scared. When I heard that Ben Coulter had been shot I knew that Juan had come back to take his revenge. It must have been Juan, no one else would dare to kill a Coulter."

But how in hell had Laredo got free of the stake-out, wondered Cade. Broken loose? The Coulters would have hog-tied him so tight it would have needed a Bowie knife to have cut through the bonds. Someone roaming the badlands at that time of night? Didn't make sense.

"And you saw nothing the night they were caught?"

"Nothing, senor. Just heard Ben and Kit but couldn't make out what they were saying. I was terrified."

47

"Miss Lucinda cry out?"

Maria shook her head.

"I didn't hear her, but she might have done."

"Did you see her after Juan was taken?"

"Oh no, I was sent to my room and early next morning Jess Coulter drove me into town."

"And you haven't spoken to her since?"

"No."

Why had Lucinda taken such an incredible risk? She must have known what Adam's reaction would have been if caught. Not a Mexican born was good enough for his daughter. The intimacy of her bedroom too irresistible? A daredevil nature? Or what? Had she cried 'rape' when caught, to avoid her father's wrath, or tried to defend her lover?

Maria cut across his train of thought.

"Please," she implored, "Don't help these people. Don't go after Juan. *Por favor, senor* . . . I — I have savings — you can have it all but please do not go after Juan."

"Maria, if I don't bring in Laredo someone else will. The Coulters won't rest now that Ben's been killed. They'll hire another bounty hunter or maybe even a posse, but they'll get him."

"You wouldn't turn him over to the Coulters?"

"For another stake-out? No way. Someone's got to talk to Laredo, tell him to quit killing before he's caught. Sure, he's justified in seeking revenge, but it cannot go on. He should make for the border pronto. Leastways he's got one Coulter scalp under his belt."

Maria said: "He's proud, senor — proud: he'll not listen to you."

"He's got to," growled Cade. "All I know about him is that he's tall for a Mexican and has a finger missing. What else, Maria?"

She launched into such a detailed, enthusiastic description of Laredo, Cade could have picked him out in a thousand. Obviously he had made a deep impression on the girl with his Latin charm and compelling blue eyes.

49

"It's Ben Coulter's funeral tomorrow," she went on. "You don't think Juan will try to kill any more of the Coulters? Adam seldom leaves the ranch and it would be a chance for him."

"With the whole town around?" Cade leaned over and lightly patted her cheek. "Quit worrying, gal. Now I've got to buy me a burro and some provisions. I'll leave town after the funeral."

Maria reached out impulsively and took his hand, her big brown eyes mirroring concern. *"Vaya con Dios,"* she breathed.

4

PREACHERS, like law enforcement officers, were as rare as hens' teeth in the cattle town of Durward, and the Coulters had great difficulty in finding one to give Ben a decent Christian burial until Jess remembered Holy Joe, an unfrocked priest, and he was dragged by his scrawny neck from the brothel next to the 'Western Star'. Appreciating his hour of glory, Joe quickly sobered, donned black clothes, and boarded the open wagon which was to convey Ben's coffin to the hillside cemetery on the outskirts of town.

All Durward turned out to watch the funeral in the hope that they might see the legendary Coulters. They were not disappointed.

Adam, haughty and disdainful, rode in the first buggy behind the wagon, with Lucinda by his side. She was in black, as befitted the occasion, but in no way did it detract from her flawless beauty. In the second buggy was Martha, also in black, accompanied by a solemn-faced Jess. Nell James in the crowd gave him an enthusiastic wave, which he studiously ignored. Kit, astride a restless chestnut, flanked the buggies with watchful eyes.

Speculation was rife as to who had shot down Ben Coulter and for what reason but no one really knew.

Holy Joe performed his duties with gusto. Ben was laid to rest next to his mother, and the buggies headed towards the Two Bar X. The crowd broke up and meandered back to town feeling they had been robbed. It had all been something of an anticlimax, though all agreed that seeing Lucinda Coulter had been worth the effort.

Kit was stuffing notes into Holy Joe's eager hand when Cade reined in alongside him. Kit swung round in surprise but waited until Joe had shuffled out of earshot. Before he could speak, Cade said curtly, "I'm going after Laredo."

"Made up your mind, huh?"

"Yep."

"Without agreeing terms?"

"Not till I've hooked the fish."

Kit shrugged. "I'll tell the boss. When are you pulling out?"

"Sundown," replied Cade, taking up the reins and setting off for town.

Kit watched him go, cast a lingering look at Ben's grave, and cantered after the buggies rolling towards the ranch. Reaching them, he went on ahead until he was almost at the ranch's southern line-camp when he sharply drew rein.

Buzzards b'God, a flock of them, screeching, squawking, squabbling in the timber to his right.

Edging his whinnying mount nearer, Kit withdrew his saddle-gun and fired a volley of shots. Startled, the scavengers created even more hideous din as they darkened the sky with their flapping wings.

Kit rode further into the woods, then froze in the saddle. His stomach heaved. Nailed to a tree sagged Slim Jackson, the ranch foreman, a sheath-knife sticking in his gut. He had no eyes. The buzzards had worked well and quickly.

As the sun sank lower in the west and the shades of night began merging to form the darkness of another velvety evening, Cade rode steadfastly out of town with the heavily-laden burro in his wake. From an upstairs window in the 'Silver Dollar' Maria watched him leave, a silent prayer on her lips.

Part Two

5

Three of a Kind

SEVERAL months before Cade Forster foiled the raid on Stein's Bank in the cattle town of Durward, an ill-assorted trio were wending their way under cover of darkness through the foothills of the Sierras, and in their train was a string of horses, cavalry mounts, each with a sheathed carbine attached to the saddle.

Delaney, the only name by which he was known, led the tortuous way through the outcropping of granite, and behind him rode Emma Carson, slumped in the saddle with hours of weary trekking. Bringing up the rear with baleful eyes fixed on Emma was Scarface Joe Mitchell. His thoughts were sour.

Why in God's name had Delaney to tote this woman around with him? All

women were bad medicine, and this
one in particular. The sooner he quit
Delaney and teamed up again with
the Galton brothers the better. From
the moment Delaney had swaggered
through the batwings of the 'Lucky
Strike' in San Ferento and spotted Emma
behind the bar he had been hooked.
Dark curls, dancing eyes and a tinkling
merry laugh. She had equally been taken
with him. The way his chestnut-coloured
hair poked rebelliously from beneath his
hat, the clear blue eyes and ready smile
showing even white teeth. His entire
air was one of supreme confidence but
with a casualness wholly alluring. A
more discerning girl than Emma Carson
would have questioned his attitude but
she was too smitten by his dashing good
looks. When she learned later that he
made his dinero from robbing banks
and saloons it only enhanced him in
her eyes. To Mitch's disgust, she quit
the saloon and teamed up with the pair
of them in their skulduggery.

Mitch liked women, but only for an

evening or a night. Taking one on the trail was asking for trouble. But he clung to Delaney; the guy was smart, cool-headed and could shade a man faster than any he knew. The way he handled his shooting-irons was a joy to see. And he could plan a raid with the precision of a military man, not a detail overlooked. How else had he managed to escape a hanging? No, sticking with Delaney had a lot to commend it, but that woman . . .

Emma intensely disliked Mitch but did not show it. She had no intention of alienating Delaney's feelings towards her. He was her life. But there were times when she could hardly contain herself. That scarred face, the wing of coarse hair falling into his piggy eyes and the perpetual leer on his thick lips. Saliva had a habit of gathering in one corner of his down-twisted mouth. When she sloped off into the bush to relieve herself, the leer would deepen and he would whistle softly through his tobacco-stained teeth. Once, when

Delaney was out scouting the land, he had 'accidentally' touched her breast when reaching for his blanket-roll. She had flared, threatening him with a knife, and he had just managed to calm her down before Delaney returned. More than once she had considered quitting the pair of them and heading for home but Delaney drew her like a magnet. If only he could make a really big haul and bid farewell to this nomadic existence.

Delaney, picking his way through the rockpiles, only had thoughts of reaching Indian Sam's shack before daybreak, do a deal with him, get rid of the mounts and be on his way. Already there were fingers of light in the sky and the primordial shapes of the night were beginning to resolve themselves into familiar sights.

Dry-gulching those pony-soldiers yesterday had been a lucky break.

Scouting ahead of Emma and Mitch, he had come across them bivouacking by an arroyo in a shallow valley. A sergeant and five troopers huddled round a dutch oven making a meal. Staked nearby were their mounts, munching away at the coarse yellow grass.

Delaney hadn't hesitated. Haring back to Mitch and Emma he had ordered the girl to lie low, then he and Mitch had crept up on the troopers. Drawing a bead on the sergeant, his white chevrons showing starkly against the blue of his tunic, Delaney dropped him with a single shot. The troopers bounded like startled rabbits for cover but the outlaws were far too quick for them. Those who had not been killed outright were writhing in their death agonies.

The pair left cover with guns at the ready, saw that all were either dead or dying, and went to calm the horses straining at their stakes. When they had ceased whinnying, Delaney ran to the oven and booted it, then withdrew his knife. He looked over his shoulder at Mitch.

"Move fast," he snarled.

Mitch stared at him.

"Move, I said."

Realisation dawned on Mitch and he

went pale. Delaney was down on his knees beside the sergeant, the knife blade flashing in the sun. Two expert strokes and the sergeant's scalp was lifted. Delaney pounced on another twitching corpse, eyes alight with excitement.

Mitch joined in the butchery unwillingly. He'd got the idea; make the killing of the troopers look like the work of Apaches to keep other pony-soldiers off their backs. Smart hombre, Delaney.

The grisly work finished, they wiped clean their knives and rounded up the cavalry horses, noting with satisfaction the sheathed carbines, an added bonus.

Before leaving the scene, Delaney made a fire of the collected scalps.

Emma had heard the firing and was waiting for them. When she saw that the string of horses were cavalry mounts, she went white.

"Have you gone loco? They're military! They'll have every trooper out of Fort Jackson searching for them."

"And they'll find them if you stick around here gabbling your goddam head off," yelled Delaney. "Get mounted — we're making for the hills."

"The hills?" Emma was appalled. Already tired, they were at least a day's ride.

"Move your goddam ass, woman. We've no time for parley. Mitch, you take the rear and keep your eyes open. Okay then, let's go."

The column moved off, Mitch sniggering to himself. Emma was scared stiff and that pleased him. She had no idea that when troopers found the bodies of their comrades they would be on the look-out for some Apache war-party and not a pair of outlaws. It was inconceivable that white men would have mutilated their own kin. Mitch wondered how she would have reacted had she known. He knew that Delaney was mean, but not so mean as to actually enjoy the butchery. He regarded Emma with renewed interest. Did she enjoy Delaney's sadism in other ways? The thought intrigued him.

Mile after mile the column plodded its way across the wide expanse of plain with

Delaney in the lead and when darkness fell entered the rounded foothills of the Sierras with the dilapidated shack of Indian Sam their goal.

The sudden crowing of a cock jogged Emma out of her stupor, goose-pimpling her flesh. She looked up with a start. Was that heap of rotted wood ahead of them Sam Trenker's shack? Rising from the arid earth it looked like a jagged stump in a hag's mouth.

"Almost there," said Delaney over his shoulder, and she could hear the relief in his voice.

The shack stood at the head of a long draw, backgrounded by a line of straggling juniper bush. By a water-hole near its entrance was a brokendown buckboard, a log with an axe embedded and among the wood chippings a scattering of hens. A galvanised iron bucket hung from a rusty nail in the door of the shack.

The column drew in and the scowl on Mitch's face deepened as he watched

Delaney dismount and amble up to the door. If the shack was anything to go by he was damned if he could see how its occupant could be of help.

Delaney rapped on the door with the butt of his gun:

"Open up, you old sourdough, it's me — Delaney."

"Who's thar?" quavered a weak voice.

"Wash some of that dirt out of your ears, and listen. It's Delaney — come on, open up."

The door swung back on its rusty hinges.

"Delaney, did you say? What in hell are you adoin' in these here parts?"

"Sam, you aim to let us in, or do we have to kick our way in?"

"Okay, okay — keep your hair on. Still kinda dark, watch where you're puttin' your feet."

Emma, even more apprehensive than Mitch, got down off her horse and almost staggered into the shack. The moment she entered she was struck by the dank smell of decayed leaves. Mitch spat

65

expressively and followed her inside.

Sam was hovering over an oil lamp and suddenly the gloom dispelled. He straightened, then peered at Emma. His eyes widened.

"That thar's a female," he said wrathfully.

"A lady, Sam," said Delaney.

"A goddam fe-male. You knows I don't hold with females in my shack. An' her wearin' breeks an' all."

Snapped Mitch, "Quit belly-aching, sourdough, and make with the coffee. Do you good to look at a real woman. She's no papoose-carrying squaw."

Delaney rounded on him sharply.

"Belt up, Mitch."

Sam gave Mitch a searching look.

"Gunslinger with a scar. Two-three weeks back had me a big hombre askin' questions about a gunslinger with a scar. Real big, looked like he could handle himself. Me, I'd say he was a bounty hunter. Cade Forster. Heard of him?"

"Forster!" exclaimed Mitch, and Sam chuckled at the fear he had aroused.

"Del — the horses," spoke up Emma wearily.

Delaney grabbed hold of Sam's arm and dragged him away from Mitch.

"Come on, old-timer: take a look-see at what I've roped in."

When the pair left Emma gazed round the shack with quivering nostrils. The floor was hard earth worn smooth by the tread of moccasined feet, and on the walls deer hides were stretched. In one corner by a cobwebbed pile of junk was a miscellany of reed baskets filled with corn, berries and beans. Littering the ground beneath the rickety table were leg bones of deer which had been fashioned into tools for dressing animal skins, and shielding the iron stove was a roughly-hewn Indian loom; on it, stretched taut, was an almost completed rug of intricate design depicting all the shapes of Nature — the roundness of the sun, the triangular shape of mountains, and the rippling pattern of water.

Indian influence had been no less

manifest in the man himself with his fringed buckskin and moccasined feet. He was small, wizened, and as tough as teak. He reeked of an earthy pungent smell. Malignancy lurked in his sunken, whiskey-coloured eyes like a toad beneath a stone and he bore loyalty to no man, red or white. In his day he had been a cavalry scout, trader and Indian-fighter but had settled down to a hermit-like existence carrying on a lucrative, nefarious trade with the Apaches. Few knew of Sam Trenker's business Delaney was one. Emma didn't like him, and wanted to leave as soon as she had rested, sentiments shared by sullen-faced Mitch.

"A big haul, Sam: half a dozen mounts with carbines. We can do a deal?"

Light was expanding rapidly and the cavalry horses, strung out in line and waiting patiently with true military discipline, were clearly visible. Sam eyed each one in turn, nodding with approval, then dragged one of the carbines from its sheath. Lovingly he stroked the dark mahogany of the stock, crooning softly to himself in a manner which greatly irritated Delaney. "Well?"

"Oh, we'll get a good price for this lot," murmured Sam. "Got me a war-party acomin' in at sundown tomorrow an' I won't take nothin' less than nuggets for them. Where are you headin' for now? Mesa?"

"Yes."

"Can you make it back in say three days from now?"

"Sure can. Same percentage as before?"

"You've got a deal. Er — Delaney . . . "

"Yeh?"

"Covered your tracks okay?"

Delaney laughed shortly.

"Reckon the military will have sore asses hunting down a war-party that don't exist."

Sam sniggered. "Allus said you was the best in the business. Okay, let's mosey inside. Guess you could use a mug of coffee. Delaney!"

"Yeh?"

"Like I say, you're the best in the business. But if'n you want to stay that way I'd drop the guy with the scar. That thar bounty hunter sure meant business. Sure as God made little apples he'll catch up with him an' it won't be healthy bein' in his company. Drop him afore it's too late. The fe-male too . . ."

"Did you say coffee, Sam?"

Sam shrugged.

"Okay," he sighed. "You'll learn."

Inside the shack Emma lay curled up on a rug near the pot-bellied stove fast asleep while Mitch dozed with his broad back propped against a wall, thick legs stuck straight out in front of him. His hat had been cast aside and the flickering flame of the oil lamp, gleaming with a pale intensity, played on his balding, ridged head. Thick black hair sprouted through the lacings of his buckskin charro jacket.

Sam shuffled over to the stove to make a meal of coffee and flapjacks and Mitch opened his eyes. "All okay?" he asked Delaney.

"Yeh, but keep your voice down — let her sleep a while longer."

"Trail ain't no place for a female," grumbled Mitch, fishing in his pocket for the makings of a smoke. "When we haulin' ass out of here?"

"Soon as you've filled your belly," Sam retorted.

Mitch glared at him. "Watch it, sourdough."

Delaney said nothing but his scowl was expressive and Mitch thought "the hell with you. Sooner I team up again with the Galtons the better."

Sam soon had the meal prepared and as Delaney and Mitch wolfed it down he went out to water the horses and collect the carbines. Emma stirred in her sleep then stretched and yawned. She sat up, rubbing her eyes. Delaney set a mug of steaming-hot coffee by her side and murmured, "Wake up, gal; there's some food for you. We'll be hitting the trail for Mesa soon as you are good and ready."

Fighting against fatigue, Emma drank and ate and the meal went some way to restoring her strength. When she had finished, she longed to lie back and close her eyes again but, just as anxious as the others to quit the evil-smelling place, struggled to her feet.

Indian Sam came shuffling back, puffing contentedly on a corncob pipe.

"If you wanna keep the hair on the top of your head, take the trail to San José and then Mesa," he advised Delaney.

"Comanche or Apache?"

"Neither," grunted Sam. "Hopi. War-party 'bout a hundred strong passed by a couple of days ago."

"Hopi, eh? Now what's upsetting them coyotes?"

Sam relit his pipe and snorted:

"What's allus upsettin' them. Goddam bandits arustlin' their beef. 'Sides, it's gettin' close to their Snake Dance time an' they allus gets excited. Hopi is like rattlers, I allus say — leave 'em alone an' they'll leave you alone. Take the trail to San José an' keep your thatch."

"Thanks, old-timer. Well — three days then?"

"I'll be awaitin'," said Sam.

The three took their leave of the old Indian trader and by noon were out of the foothills and on to the plain heading first for San José and then Mesa. All around rolled a wild scenic beauty whose chief characteristics were space, grass, and cloudless sky. Heat waves danced and by an upthrust ledge of a rockpile a coyote slunk by. On the skyline they caught sight of the swinging lazy movement of a watchful buzzard. They rode in silence, Mitch plagued by thoughts of a gun-toting bounty hunter.

Skirting the motley collection of shacks and cabins comprising San José, the trio picked up the Mesa trail as the sun was beginning to set, etching their elongated jogging shadows against the now stony terrain. Another three hours of relentless riding and the twinkling lights of the town could be seen like a myriad welcoming beacons.

Emma was pleased with the choice of Mesa. Bigger than most of the frontier towns, it had more to offer. The only drawback was that it had a marshal stalking its high-boarded sidewalks — George Ulysses Rowntree, shotgun in the crook of his arm and a fierce determination to swing all outlaws from the nearest cottonwood.

They reined in at the 'Golden Nugget' and Delaney went in to book rooms. Checking in at the reception desk he paid no attention to the Mexican in a corner seat, eyeing him with keen interest.

Delaney and Emma took one room and Mitch another. They were soon asleep, undisturbed by the clamour from the bar below.

6

DELANEY had too mercurial a disposition for Emma to be supremely content in the days that followed for in one moment he would be passionate and tender and in the next sardonic, brooding and restless. Scrubbed clean of trail-dust and wearing the most provocative dresses she could buy, she did her utmost to captivate him entirely and there were times when she thought she had succeeded, then, almost at the point of triumph, he would walk out on her with some curt remark. God knew where he went to, the nearest brothel or poker game, no doubt. The best time had been when he returned from Sam Trenker's shack with enough nuggets to buy the three of them all the liquor and enjoyment they desired and they had lived life to the full. The old scoundrel had done a good deal with the hostiles, greedy for guns and horses, and trust in him had paid off. Delaney knew that it would. Indian Sam's life depended on trust by outlaw and redskin. In those days even Joe Mitchell seemed to enjoy himself and there was less talk of the Galtons but now the money was beginning to run out and anxiety was colouring their different moods. Delaney's increasing bouts of silence with outbursts of choleric temper made Emma draw within herself and more than ever she was seen with a gin bottle in her hand. Mitch relapsed into his usual sullen self and took himself off to other saloons in the town to drown his gloomy thoughts in whiskey. Then, when all were at their lowest ebb, Mitch staggered back to the 'Golden Nugget', his piggy eyes gleaming with excitement. Delaney and Emma were stretched out on the bed. With a cheroot dangling from the corner of his mouth he looked utterly bored and she was so far soaked in drink she didn't even bother to either button up her blouse or cover her shapely legs, even though the intruder was Mitch.

Delaney propped himself up on his elbows, smoke screwing his eyes to pinpoints. Mitch was usually more solemn than an Indian brave so something momentous must have triggered him off. Even his scar, livid down his left cheek, was twitching. Delaney waited in that aggravatingly detached way he had.

"Mort Jacoby's in town, the skinny guy who helped us pull the Mason City job. Made a beeline for me as soon as he saw me. He's playing for mighty high stakes and wants to cut us in."

Delaney swung his legs off the bed and doused his cheroot.

"What stakes, Mitch?"

"The Overland."

Delaney stared.

"Sounds crazy but listen: Mort's in cahoots with a guy who works for the line — Ned Kramer — and it's his idea only he needs help. Mort's willing, but it needs more than two to pull the job."

"Only guys I knew who dry-gulched

a stage got their necks stretched," said Delaney drily.

"Yeh, but was one of their party riding shotgun?"

"Shotgun?"

Mitch slapped his thigh with glee.

"Kramer rides shotgun," he said triumphantly.

Delaney whistled softly. With one of their party riding back-stage the job had possibilities, great possibilities.

Mitch straddled a chair and pushed his eager face close to Delaney's.

"In a couple of days' time Cole and Hargreaves are shipping most of their dinero — bullion and notes — to the bank at Culvert's Creek where they've opened up new mines and Kramer will be aboard that stage. He knows the trail to Culvert's like the back of his hand, just where to dry-gulch, how to make a getaway. It's a chance in a lifetime, Delaney. Clean up, and we're made for life."

Emma stirred and gave Mitch a glassy look. "Wha's eatin' you?" she slurred.

"Go to sleep," snapped Delaney, giving her a push and sending the gin bottle on to the floor. "How come this Kramer is all-fired het-up to pull a job like this, Mitch? Has he worked long for the stage company?"

"Just what I asked Mort. Kramer has a wife who's got ambitions and wants to make the big time. She's scratching a living on some goddam small holding just outta town and even with the money Ned makes is dissatisfied. Grumbles all day and threatens to leave him unless he does something about it. Kramer's scared stiff she walks out on him and will do anything to keep her."

"Like putting his head in a noose?" Delaney raised an eyebrow.

"Kramer's been with the company four years and knows what he's doing," said Mitch with a show of impatience. "With you running the job it's a cinch. Think of it. Kramer, riding shotgun, guns down the two front riders, so all we've got to do is take care of the guards inside the stage."

Delaney grinned wryly. "This Kramer must think a lot of his wife to run such a risk. What's she like?"

"Never seen her," grunted Mitch, casting an eye at Emma sprawled on the far side of the bed.

Delaney knew what he was thinking — jobs and females should be kept apart.

"Then it's time we did," muttered Delaney, getting to his feet. "With a job like this we should know everybody who's got a hand in it — especially if there's some filly."

Mitch looked doubtful. Sure they should know who would be taking part in the hold-up but was that the only reason why Delaney wanted to meet Kramer's wife?

"Come on, Mitch — let's go parley," said Delaney, buckling on his sideguns.

Mitch nodded at Emma. "What about her?"

Delaney shrugged. "What do you care?"

Mitch sniggered and stood up. "You can say that again, pardner."

Although he hadn't seen Mort Jacoby in

years Delaney recognised him at once. There was no mistaking that thin face with the long thrust of jaw boasting a bluish hue. A gangling hombre, his hips were so slim it was a wonder they supported his holsters. He was sitting in a downtown saloon and lost in thought but his face lit up when he saw the pair making their way towards him. He stood up to greet them, almost a token of respect for Delaney.

"Sit down, Mort — let's talk," said Delaney, drawing up a chair. God, the guy was skinnier than he remembered. The knuckles in his wrists stuck out like enlarged walnuts.

Delaney leaned forward and lowered his voice, his eyes fixed on Mort's tense face. "Mitch has given me the lowdown but I want details, then we can mosey over to the Kramers. Okay?"

"Okay, Delaney — let's talk."

For the best part of an hour the three sat huddled round the table talking in whispers and when Delaney was satisfied they left the saloon to make their way towards the Kramer holding, a ramshackle affair on the outskirts of town. Mort led the way on his mustang, over an arroyo and up a dirt track towards the cabin whose sole redeeming feature was the solid phalanx of sunflowers flanking the porchway. Pitch was peeling from the walls of the outhouses and the buggy crying out for paint. Little wonder Rachel Kramer longed to escape such desolation.

Ned was waiting for them by the open door but she was nowhere to be seen.

He was about thirty, barrel-chested and with crisp hair springing up proudly from a corrugated brow. An 'honest John' thought Delaney — would he have the guts to cold-bloodedly gun down his fellow riders? Must be desperate to please and keep this wife of his. And by the same token she must be some woman to make him do it. More than ever Delaney wanted to meet her.

The four were quickly down to business and were putting the finishing touches to their plan when Rachel came in through the back door. Ned sprang to his feet. "Come on in, honey," he cried. "Meet the boys. You know Mort and this here is Joe Mitchell. And this is — "

"Delaney."

He turned in his chair with a slight smile and nodded. "Pleased to make your acquaintance, ma'am."

She wore typical homesteader dress, sunbonnet and voluminous calico frock, and her face though deeply tanned was smooth, rounded and free of the usual lines inflicted by the intense Arizonian sun. Delaney sensed an animal lust in her which struck a responsive chord in him but if she was impressed by his looks she certainly didn't show it. She cast aside her bonnet and a mass of red hair tumbled about her neck and shoulders.

"Everything set?" Her voice was low and husky.

"Yes," enthused Ned. "We want you to load the buggy with all the food you can find and Delaney will take you to a hide-out he knows. When we pull the job we make for this place and lie low until everything dies down. Then we split up and go our different ways. Okay?"

"Makes sense. Where is this hide-out?"

Ned looked at Delaney who replied, "Three or four miles along the Santa Fé trail. A cave in the hills. Nothing much, but safe."

"When do we start?" she asked.

"Here and now."

The daunting prospects of two nights alone in a hillside cave seemed not to dismay her and she immediately set about preparing for the journey. Mitch rode back to town with Mort while Ned began clearing up the holding and slaughtering the few chickens. Rachel changed into trail clothes and the transformation delighted Delaney but he passed no comment. The blanket shirt clung seductively to her shapely bosom and the cowpuncher hat, thrust back on her head, gave her a boyish air at variance with her cold, calculating eyes.

When all was ready, Ned gave her a

parting hug and she climbed up into the laden buggy and took up the reins. Delaney rode ahead and the buggy jerked into life and rolled after him.

The evening was well advanced by the time they reached the bleak remote cavern and the shades of night were beginning to creep down the hillsides. Somewhere in the distance a coyote howled mournfully and a shiver ran down Rachel's back. Manoeuvring the buggy along the mountain ledges had taxed her strength and she was pleased the ordeal was over. Delaney quickly unharnessed the buggy horse and, after unloading, sent the buggy over the ledge and watched it career down the ravine in an avalanche of stone and shale. It was some time before the echoes of the crash died and the hills again wrapped themselves in an eerie silence. Meanwhile Rachel had made the inside of the cave as comfortable as possible with blankets strewn everywhere and an oil lamp perched on top of a wooden box. She made no effort to speak until she was satisfied, then turned to Delaney with a questioning look in her eyes.

They had scarcely spoken a dozen words between them since they met but their minds were so finely attuned speech was unnecessary. He just took her in his arms, laid her on one of the blankets, and her response was so eager, so overwhelmingly satisfying, that in those moments Delaney knew that it was the end of the trail for Emma. He still had great need of her however. So explosive an operation as holding up the Overland Stage needed a second more permanent hide-out and that was where he would persuade her to take her part. The future could take care of itself.

7

DELANEY, crouching in a rockpile overlooking the deep, narrow gorge, caught the distant rhythmic drumming of horses' hooves, and as he reached for his saddle-gun signalled to Mitch on the far side.

Dead on time, the stagecoach rounded the bend and entered the gorge, and the outlaws had a clear view of the straining horses and swaying coach with Ned Kramer on his vigilant rear perch.

Delaney focused on the galloping team, waiting tensely for Kramer's shots. The moment they rang out, he began pumping white-hot lead at the horses, bringing them to their knees with ear-splitting squeals and catapulting the stage over the struggling mass.

Mitch's hawk eyes were fixed on the upturned stage and anyone who might move. Kramer, poor dupe, was dead, his neck broken when hurled to the ground. And he had obligingly accounted for the two riding up front, but who was inside the coach?

The pair scrambled down the sides of the gorge and approached the stage with guns at the ready. One wheel had been smashed beyond repair and the other was spinning ludicrously. The dust was beginning to settle and they peered inside. Two men, one dead and the other badly hurt, a moustachioed old-timer no longer fit for riding shotgun. He gazed up at them in hurt wonder, trying to dislodge the pile of boxes pinning him to what was once the top of the coach. Mitch, his nerves rubbed raw by the squeals of the dying horses, blasted the old man's head off his shoulders, then turned to Delaney. "Where in hell's Jacoby?"

As though in answer, Mort came galloping up the gorge with a string of mounts in his wake, each with empty saddle-bags. The three lost no time in shooting off the locks of each box and stuffing the contents into the bags and when all was taken Delaney took the lead and guided them towards the cave where Rachel waited.

When she saw that Ned was not among the group, her eyes opened in mock horror. Delaney put on an excellent charade of gravely informing her of his death and she put on an even better one in accepting the news. Both knew that it had never been intended that Ned Kramer would survive the hold-up. Had he not inadvertently broken his neck Delaney would have shot him as easily as he had the stage's front riders. Mort, who had not seen what happened, loudly sympathised with Rachel, but Mitch, knowing Delaney, was highly suspicious but said nothing.

Flushed with success, the gang settled down to their enforced stay in the cavern, always on the look-out, but the crowding and inactivity soon palled and Mort was itching to be on his way. Mitch shared his feelings but decided to stick with Delaney who seemed to have the knack of pulling off any job. When at last Mort defiantly said he was quitting, Delaney, surprisingly, made no effort to stop him. Secretly he was glad to see the back of Mort Jacoby, a much more intelligent man than Mitch, one who could be hard to handle. He took with him his share of the loot and was well satisfied.

In the next few days when Mitch was on look-out and out of earshot, Delaney took Rachel to one side and discussed their future plans. She was taken aback when told about Emma but he soon allayed her fears in his eloquent way and assured her that as soon as it was prudent to leave the second hide-out Emma would be ditched and Mitch could go his own way. Rachel was dubious. Why this second hide-out at San Felipe? And why such a godforsaken town? With ill-concealed irritation, Delaney again explained. Posses would be combing the hillsides for weeks, maybe months to come and it was essential that they laid low and Emma would have a place ready for them, stocked with provisions. Jacoby had taken his chances but certain-sure he was already swinging from some tree. San Felipe? Sure it was a ghost town, which was why he had chosen it. Once it had been as prosperous as Mason City and Mesa but the gold reefs had soon worked out and the town died. Now there was not too much life round and plenty of abandoned shacks since the diggers quit. Emma would have had no trouble in finding a suitable place. Mollified to a certain extent, Rachel relapsed into a sulky silence. The conditions in the cavern had reached intolerable proportions and did nothing to improve her mood. She had been here longer than any of them and the strain was beginning to tell. The monotonous diet, the stink of the horses and worst of all no love-making, not with that scar-faced gunslinger always hanging around. The loot, with its untold potentialities, only made matters worse. There it lay, the key to a life of unbelievable pleasure, taunting and mocking her. Although prepared to stick it out two or three days longer Delaney decided to quit, realising that both Rachel and Mitch had been stretched to the limit. "Another day," grunted Mitch, "and we would be up to our goddam knees in horse crap." He'd rubbed along okay with Rachel, better than Emma, maybe on account of those glorious breasts which she did little to hide, and marvelled at Delaney putting the women in the same corral.

From a distant hill one pair of eyes watched the party emerge from the cavern and into the sunlight. He lay flat on his stomach hugging the arid ground, with the sun's rays forcing their way through his blanket shirt and irritating his scarred back.

8

ALONG the rutted road trundled the buckboard, past adobe houses where squatted blanket-draped peons, and into the main part of the town slumbering in the heat of the noonday sun. Few spared the plump, grimy woman driving so much as a glance, and Emma was content. She loathed the disguise but could not risk prospective beaux chasing her and prying into her business. Fortunately the owner of the feed and grain store was as stupid as a mule, otherwise he would have questioned the large amounts of provisions she bought. Thank God this should be the last day. Tomorrow he would be here. And Mitch, worse luck.

So it would be the three of them again but not, she hoped, for long. Mitch could take his share of the loot and vamoose forever.

Two days ago a posse had ridden into town questioning everyone so she knew that the job had been pulled off, but had Delaney escaped? One more day and she would know. The days and hours had crawled by since she last saw him and she was eaten with impatience.

Leaving behind the sleepy, derelict town, she drove on into the plain with its abandoned shacks, mute testimony to the once thriving community towards their rendezvous, a cabin in the lee of the ruins of an old Mexican fort. Here and there the remains of mine workings still gashed and marred the plain.

When she reached the cabin she sat for a while, staring at it malignantly. How she loathed the place with its creaking doors, ill-fitting floor planks and rough, hand-made furniture. She recalled the first day she had seen it; how she had made herself twig brooms and gone to work on the piled-up dust, making the place as presentable as possible.

Presently she got down from the buckboard, unharnessed the horse, and carried her latest bag into the cabin, setting it in a corner with the rest of the food. Sweating freely, she sat down for a few moments then stirred herself. Taking up a bucket, she splashed water into a blue enamel basin, then, about to wash, caught sight of herself in the cracked mirror nailed to the wall. God, what a sight! She pulled a face at her reflection. After a thorough wash she turned again to the bed but saw a cur slinking by the open doorway. She was about to chase it when she saw how bony its ribs were and instead threw it a few scraps. As the dog bounded eagerly after the food she took her foot and slammed shut the door.

Sitting on the edge of the bed she mechanically unbuttoned her flowing dress and began pulling out all the padding which had so effectively disguised her, and when it was piled on the wooden floor gave it a vicious kick. She stared moodily at it for some moments then carried on undressing and when most of her clothing lay crumpled at her feet she sank back on the bed with a sigh and reached out for the bottle of gin.

Should she? Ah, the hell with it: many lonely hours ahead until tomorrow, and she'd be okay when he got here. Sure, she would be. She put the bottle to her lips, tilted it, and drank deeply. God, but that was good. Her eyes began to glow, thinking of his return, and she felt her whole body aching with desire. As the desire grew stronger she kindled it with an alcoholic lust until the gin, aided by the afternoon sun, sent her into a drunken stupor. There she lay with tightly closed eyes and sprawling limbs as the afternoon dragged on and the shades of evening crept into the cabin.

Arriving at the rendezvous in the gathering dusk a day earlier than anticipated, Delaney had no difficulty in locating it with such a landmark as the old Mexican fort. The familiar buckboard stood by the door but there was no light in the cabin and the party approached with caution. There was no sound but the plodding of hooves. The crenellated outlines of the fort, stark against the evening sky, came ever nearer. When they reached the cabin they drew rein. Delaney dismounted and went up td the door. It was shut but opened surprisingly at his touch. He peered in, saw Emma stretched out on the bed. On the floor by her side an empty bottle glinted. He ran his eye around the room. Food and drink was everywhere. Emma had done her work well. He turned back to the others. "She's here all right. Mitch, unload the horses and get them under cover inside the fort. We'll carry the loot inside."

Mitch said, "Is she asleep?"

"Yes. Come on, Rachel: down you get. It's been a hell of a long day."

Asleep, thought Mitch, drunk you mean. There was trouble ahead, he knew it. Question was how soon would it start. Delaney was out of his cotton-picking mind.

Delaney and Rachel stood side by side

looking down on her. They exchanged glances.

She murmured: "Better wake her up."

"Wonder if a posse's been through," said Delaney.

"Won't know till you've roused her. God, what a stink!"

"We'll waken her but do like I say. It's only for a few days."

Rachel shrugged.

Schooled by Delaney into accepting her role towards Emma and hating it, Rachel consoled herself with thoughts of future wealth. But it was going to be damned hard watching this woman kiss and fondle her Del and act as though nothing had happened. Even in the gloom Rachel could see that she was an attractive woman. Suddenly she didn't want to be around when he wakened her. Moreover the stale odour of drink and urine, trapped within the cabin walls, was getting to her.

"I'll lend a hand with the horses," she said, adding significantly, "Leave the door open."

Incensed at finding Emma like this Delaney fought to control his temper. He must avoid a row with her until he was good and ready to leave.

He drew the dusty curtains and lit the oil lamp, keeping the wick low. Small lizards scuttled across the floor to disappear among the stacked flour bags. Emma's mouth was open and there were dark stains on her underclothes in the region of her groin. Delaney threw a blanket over her in case the others came in sooner than expected then got some water and a cloth and dabbed Emma's face.

"For Chrissake wake up," he hissed.

She stirred and moaned.

"Wake up, damn it."

Her eyes flickered.

"Emma — wake up."

Dim though the light was, it hurt her eyes.

"Del!" she gasped, struggling to sit up.

He grasped her shoulders tightly and shook her.

"Emma, has a posse been through?"

"Posse?"

"Yes God damn it — a posse. Has a posse been through?"

She got him into focus then cast her eyes about. He knew she was looking around for the bottle and his temper flared. He tightened his grip on her to such a degree that his knuckles shone white.

"Stop," she yelled, "you're hurting me."

"Has there been a posse — answer me."

"Yes, damn it, yes — couple of days ago, then they vamoosed." She was fully awake now, rubbing her released shoulders. "What in hell's the matter with you anyway? When did you get back?"

Delaney sank back with a sigh of relief. So they had searched the area and found nothing. Good. But they would have to keep a look-out. That fort was ideal for keeping watch. It commanded a magnificent view over the surrounding plain.

"Just ridden in." He took his eyes off the deep bruising of her shoulders and looked round the cabin. "You've done a good job, Emma," he said approvingly, then, with a hint of apology, "I had to know about the posse. It's been a long haul and nothing must go wrong now."

"Well they've been and gone," said Emma, tossing back her curls and rubbing sleep from her eyes. "Job go okay?"

"Like taking candy off a kid. Only Kramer got killed. Got thrown from the stage. Jacoby quit the cave after a few days but Mitch and Rachel are here seeing to the loot and the horses. Emma — you should get an eyeful of that dinero — "

"Rachel?" she snapped. "Just who in hell's Rachel?"

"Kramer's wife, who else?"

"You've never spoken of him having a wife."

"Why the hell should I? Kramer wasn't going to leave his wife behind, was he? She had no part in the job but

101

we couldn't leave her after Kramer was killed."

Emma said accusingly: "So you've been holed up with her this past week."

"And with Mitch and a half dozen mounts," retorted Delaney. "Now cut the crap, Emma, it's been a long day. How's about rustling up some food and coffee?"

Delaney felt a twinge of unease. Had he been over-confident? Underestimated Emma? The girl was no fool. She was thinking: four guys set out to rob the stage and only one of them had been killed, the one who had a wife. What was she like.

She got up from the bed unsteadily and Delaney put his arm around her.

"It's been a long time, honey, but as soon as this dies down we'll have all the time in the world. And all the money you need. Now how about something to eat? I'm starving."

Emma looked up at him.

"Is — is she pretty?" she asked uncertainly.

Delaney slapped her playfully, then kissed her.

"I've seen burros that are prettier. Come on, gal — food."

There was struggling in the doorway and Mitch came staggering in with leather saddlebags under his brawny arms. He set them down with a grunt, pushed back his hat and blew out his cheeks. "Horses seen to. Where do we stash this lot?"

"By the window. Where's Mrs Kramer?"

Mrs Kramer? No longer Rachel, huh? Mitch got the swing of it.

"Bringing in the rest." Mitch looked at Emma. "Howdy."

Emma merely nodded. She always had difficulty in talking to him. Thank God she would soon be seeing the last of him. There was more scuffling in the doorway and Rachel came puffing in with two more saddlebags. Delaney, holding himself in check, made no move to help her. Mitch grinned. Already Delaney was fooling Emma. What a contrast to the past few days when he had rushed to help

Rachel in all matters, however small.

Rachel set down the bags by the others and straightened, arching her back and throwing into relief her magnificent bust. Mitch's grin broadened as he watched Delaney studiously avoid Rachel's contortions. She threw off her sombrero and shook free her mass of red hair.

"Jeez, but I'm bushed," she said.

Emma stared.

It was worse than she feared, far worse. Why this woman was — was — riveting. Her full, pouting lips, smooth-tanned cheeks and mane of glorious hair. Even her travel-stained clothing could not diminish her over-all effect. The voice was low, husky and captivating. Emma's earlier suspicions of Delaney flared, sowing deadly seeds of uncontrollable jealousy.

"Emma — meet Mrs Kramer," said Delaney with feigned nonchalance. "She's not feeling too good. Like I told you, her husband Ned was killed in the hold-up. Thrown from the stage."

How damned convenient, thought Emma. Died — but how? Someone pull a trigger on him. Delaney?

She gave Rachel the same treatment she had Mitch, a mere nod.

The meal was hardly a success so tense was the atmosphere. Delaney pretended not to notice. Mitch didn't notice. So hungry and tired he just wolfed down the meal, ignoring both women. Delaney was glad when the meal was over and the light doused. He took first watch on the fort while the others slept. Emma's dreams were far from pleasant.

After three long, hot, boring unbearable days Mitch climbed the crumbling stairs to join Delaney on the walls of the fort. Lizards scattered in all directions at his approach, burying themselves in nooks and crannies. Delaney, squinted his eyes against the sun, continued to search the plain.

"All clear?" asked Mitch, leaning heavily on the wall and gazing outwards.

Delaney dropped the butt end of his smoke and stood on it. "Yep. Hauling out now?"

Mitch gave him a sidelong glance and said guiltily, "I reckon."

"Not safe." Delaney kept his eyes on the plain.

"Posse's been and gone," argued Mitch.

"And can come back. Where you heading?"

"Durward."

"The Galtons, eh?"

"Yep."

Delaney turned to him with a wry smile. "Nothing more to say then, Mitch, except *hasta luego*."

"Not this time, Delaney — it's *adios*." Mitch fell silent, then, "What's she got on you?"

"Rachel?" He laughed shortly. "Dunno. But whatever it is she's got what it takes."

Mitch shook his head sadly. "One squaw's mighty bad medicine, but two in the same corral sure is askin' for trouble. *Adios* then, I'm haulin' ass, here an' now."

"Try the 'Silver Dollar' in Durward. Best hooch in town. Come sundown you'll be hoe-digging in the saloon . . . if you're not dangling from a rope. *Adios, amigo.*"

Delaney remained on the wall watching Mitch ride out on to the plain, his mount heavy with loot. Like Emma, like Rachel, he was glad to see the back of him.

9

JOE MITCHELL had no illusions about Delaney. Captured by some posse and about to be hanged, he would have no hesitation in denouncing Mitch as one of the gang who had dry-gulched the Overland Stage, which was why he had told him he was making for Durward. Let some tin-horn marshal ride his ass sore hunting for him around the foothills of the Sierras, he would be living it up in some burg way up north. Delaney was heading for real trouble with those two squaws and could easily end up with his neck in a noose.

Mitch's plan was as simple as the man himself. Head north, bury his share of the loot on the outskirts of some town and live life to the full as long as the wealth lasted. Useless putting it into a bank; too many questions would be asked and banks could be raided.

A couple of hard days' ride brought him to Philipville and in a stony, inhospitable draw abounding with rattlesnakes and lizards on the outskirts he found an ideal cache for his saddlebags containing his share of the loot. Taking some of the gold-dust and nuggets, he rode into town and reined in at the first barber's saloon for a much needed haircut and shave. After downing a couple of beers, he called in at a store and treated himself to a new set of duds. Hair slicked down by bear grease and reeking of cheap scent, he sauntered into the first saloon and tossed back two or three shots of raw whiskey.

Several poker games were in progress but it was the one near the batwings which drew his attention, largely because of the blonde hovering behind the thin-faced dealer in his elegant frock-coat. She was no beauty, but she had a bust to rival Rachel's and that was all that interested Mitch. He was only too well aware of his own shortcomings. His chunky figure and that scar . . .

About to light a cheroot, Mitch paused to watch one of the poker players jump to his feet, angrily slam down his cards and stalk away from the table. This was his cue. He lit the cheroot and swaggered over.

"Okay to join in?"

Ed Malone, the dealer, took him in in one glance. Some hick who had made it good, judging by his stiff new duds and expensive smoke. He shrugged and said affably, "Why not?"

Mitch drew up a chair and sat down, pushing down his holster-belt which threatened to ride up over his paunch. The blonde didn't spare him a second look.

The game continued in rapt silence and it was only when Mitch had exhausted his few dollars and began paying out in gold that the girl's eyes came to life. Mitch knew that he had caught her interest but waited some time before meeting her eyes. She flashed him a warm smile to which he responded with a ponderous wink. If Malone was aware of this laboured coquetry he didn't show it. The blonde's smiles continued and Mitch soon decided that he had had enough poker. His losses were slight and Malone raised no objection so he left the table with a significant, inviting look at the girl. He made towards the bar but stopped at the sound of her voice: "Stranger in town?"

Mitch turned. She was standing with her hands on her hips, tongue licking her carmined lips.

"Yup," he said.

"Belle Knight — welcome to Philipville. Buy me a drink?"

"Sure will, honey." Mitch grinned broadly.

Everyone in the room, including himself, knew that he was being taken for a sucker, but he didn't care. So what if she was after a quick buck?

They found a corner seat, Mitch drinking whiskey and Belle gin. She did most of the talking, which suited Mitch. Each knew what the other wanted but maintained a charade until Belle invited him to her rooms above the saloon. The more he had drunk the more boastful he had become and although she had figured him to be a man of some substance she couldn't prise out of him the source of his wealth. But she was determined, even though it would mean more than one night sharing the blankets with him.

Mitch slept most of the next day and Belle was happy to let him, bribed by one of his gold nuggets with which she bought herself a beautiful pendant. In the evening, the pair made their way downstairs to the bar where several girls noticed with envy Belle's pendant, until they got an eyeful of the guy by her side. There were limits beyond which most wouldn't go. Malone strolled by, pausing only to whisper in Belle's ear before taking up his habitual spot by the batwings. Later, when the pair were comfortably seated as on the previous night, he looked in her direction and, catching her eye, gave the slightest nod. Belle nudged Mitch.

"Ed has a chair for you."

Bored by her inconsequential chatter and eager to recoup his losses, Mitch accepted the invitation with alacrity.

There were four at the table including Malone. Mitch took up a seat opposite to him only this time Belle was hovering at his shoulder and not Malone's.

Mitch was in good form. Within a short time he had not only recouped his losses of the previous night but, to Belle's squeaks of delight, had begun piling up his winnings. Then suddenly, she squealed out "Mitch!" He glanced up from his cards, saw Malone's derringer and heard him hiss:

"Four-flusher."

In a single movement Mitch sprang to his feet, upsetting table and cards, dived for his guns and fired. Malone dropped his gun and clutching his chest fell writhing on the floor.

"Drop 'em," a voice thundered behind Mitch, and he felt something poking into his back. He craned his neck to see who was behind and the order was again barked. Mitch's guns clattered on the floor.

"Turn around."

Mitch turned. A red-necked marshal with a sawn-off shotgun. He nodded at the cards closest to Mitch's feet. "Pick 'em up."

Mitch did as he was told and the marshal took them from him. He held one to the light and growled, "Pin-pricks, you four-flushin' bastard. We don't like four-flushers in this burg. Get movin'."

"Belle Knight sent me, though God knows why."

Mitch's head shot up. In the cell doorway stood an elderly man in sombre broadcloth.

"Blackwood's the name — lawyer," he introduced himself in a dry, rasping voice. "You're in a fix, Mitchell, and Belle's asked me to do what I can for you. I guess you know the score. Day after tomorrow Judge Wetherall will be in town for trials, and if you get off you'll be the first murderer Sebastian ever let off. So there's only one thing I can do. Convince the marshal that you acted in self-defence so that he won't bring you to trial."

A gleam of hope flickered in Mitch's eyes. For three long days he had languished in this oven-hot, bug-ridden cell with the marshal's daily assurance that his stay wouldn't be long. Soon he would have all the fresh air he wanted — dangling from a tree.

Mitch said hoarsely: "Belle was behind me. She must have seen that Malone drew first."

"And the marshal will take notice of that? A woman you've been sleeping with? Bought jewellery for?"

"What about the others?"

"Guys you'd been two-timing? Why should they speak up for you?"

Bawled Mitch, "I wasn't two-timin' nobody . . . "

"They think you were," Blackwood cut across him. "Cards had pin-pricks. None of them will speak up for you unless . . . "

He stopped abruptly, scanning the other's face.

"Yeh?"

"You make it worth their while." The lawyer calmly lit a cigar, allowing time for his words to sink in. "Belle seems to think you're a man of substance, Mitchell. Can you afford to pay these guys, assuming they are prepared to swear that Malone pulled a gun on you? I should add that there's also my fee to consider."

The outcome was of course inevitable. To save his neck Mitch had to reveal the source of his wealth. The amount was sufficient to bribe the poker players and pay the lawyer. Strangely, neither the lawyer nor the marshal questioned the unusual hiding-place for the nuggets and gold-dust, a cache in a draw on the outskirts of town.

Mitch was turned loose with a dire warning never to return to Philipville. Penniless he rode south, cursing the day he set foot in the town, and headed for Durward, chancing both Delaney's possible treachery and some bounty hunter catching up with him.

He found the Galton brothers. They were in optimistic mood, discussing the prospects of a raid on Stein's Bank in Durward, a town that had no marshal.

The tap at the office door made Simon Blackwood look up sharply. "Come in," he said.

The door opened.

"Ah," said the lawyer. "I've been expecting you."

"Everything okay?"

Blackwood smiled thinly.

"Of course," he said. He pointed to a pair of small sacks on his desk. "One for Belle and one for you. You'll see she gets hers?"

"Don't I always?" countered Ed Malone, grasping both sacks.

The lawyer replied drily: "Just make sure she manages to swap blanks or some day you'll end up on a slab. Good-day to you."

10

MITCH'S premature departure meant that Delaney had to spend more time on look-out but it also provided him with an excuse to escape the pretence of affection with Emma. Moreover, the close proximity of Rachel with its unavoidable denial was an increasing source of irritation from which only the lonely hours on the walls of the fort gave sanctuary. Both women clamoured to leave the boredom of their confinement but were persuaded by his argument that it was far too dangerous. Jacoby and Mitchell, he assured them were fools. An outlaw of some repute, the women respected his judgement and ceased grumbling.

Delaney knew that his plan was working. Rachel, even though fires of resentment smouldered beneath, was continuing to play her role of studied indifference, while Emma was being encouraged to drink more. When he decided to leave, he would make sure that she would be in one of her helpless states. Once when she had been drunk Rachel and he had snatched an hour of love-making in the lee of the fort.

Emma, however, was fooling them. She had seen everything. Each time Rachel had left the cabin to answer a call of nature, Emma had substituted the gin with water, and feigned drunkenness. She was a far better actress than Rachel.

Then Emma played her trump card.

Convincing Delaney that more supplies were needed, she persuaded him to let her drive into town in her former disguise. He needed little persuasion. Time alone with Rachel was too tempting and overruled his natural caution.

The buckboard was made ready and the horse harnessed but Emma waited until he had returned to the look-out before setting off. She took her time in leaving and waved to him as she drove off.

Delaney waited until she was almost out of sight then hurried to the cabin. He flung open the door then stood stock-still. Rachel lay sprawled across the bed in a tangle of blankets, her mane of hair saturated with blood. From neck to midriff her checked shirt had been ripped open and plunged deep into her left breast was an ordinary kitchen knife thrust with all the outraged passion of a jealous woman. His eyes shot to beneath the window. The loot had gone.

Ghost town though it was San Felipe had its law enforcement officer — Ewan Butler. In its heyday, when the saloons were filled with brawling, drunken diggers, he had kept law and order with commendable ability, but now there was little to do and he was eaten with impatience awaiting his transfer to distant San José. True there had been some excitement when the posse had arrived searching for the stage robbers but that had been some days ago and the town had settled back to its usual soporific monotony.

He was sprawling in his swivel-chair with his pipe stuck in the corner of his down-twisted mouth when Emma burst in, eyes wild with terror. She'd got rid of her disguise and looked the attractive woman that she was.

Butler shot to his feet as she blurted out her story. She had been captured by the stagecoach robbers and held prisoner by them in a shack near the old Mexican fort. She and another woman — she didn't know her name. They had been repeatedly raped by the men, two of them, but they talked of others who had been in the hold-up. She'd managed to escape . . .

Butler cut through her babble. Were these guys still at the shack? Still just two of them? Where did they intend to make for when they quit? How well armed were they? Thoughts of glory, making a name for himself as the captor of stage robbers, and not least the reward that went with it, electrified him. Obtaining all the information he needed, he almost brushed Emma to one side and raced out to round up a posse.

Through his office window Emma watched the posse leave and the minute they were out of sight dashed to the buckboard and headed out of town as fast as she could go. When she thought the time appropriate, she stopped the buckboard, unhitched the horse, and slinging the bags containing some of the loot over the saddle, rode off into the blue.

Crouched low in the saddle and with shots whistling around his ears, Delaney raced for the hills with the posse in close pursuit, hell-bent on getting the reward for him. Reaching the hills, he wound and twisted his way through the valleys and gorges with superb horsemanship but was unable to shake off the relentless pursuers. Then he made the fatal mistake of entering a draw which ended in steep, unscalable shale.

Reining in, he savagely swung round

his horse's head to face the approaching posse, five in all. The saddle-gun was at his shoulder, and he prepared to sell his life dearly. Pick off as many as he could and hope to break through the rest and out of the draw.

The posse drew rein. He hadn't made for the rocks as expected but intended to charge them. What the hell, so long as they collected his boots and saddle. Grimly they awaited his attack.

Delaney had his eyes on the tin-horn marshal, the one with the star. He would be first to get it.

A deathly silence reigned in the draw, then a volley of shots rang out startling hunters and hunted. Just managing to hold his mount in check, Delaney first looked up to the top of the draw and caught sight of faint puffs of smoke, then towards the posse. All five were either dead or dying, prone on the ground or slumped in the saddle.

He could make nothing of it. All he knew was that he was safe — at least for now. Steadying his nervous mount with reassuring pats he watched in amazement as three figures scrambled down the side of the draw in a flurry of dust. Two came towards him, rifles slung over their shoulders. The third and tallest of the three ignored him and strolled over to the posse. Satisfied by what he had seen, he sauntered back to the others. "All dead, Romero: round up the horses."

The one called Romero took his eyes off Delaney. *"Si senor."*

The leader looked up at Delaney still clasping his gun.

He said: *"Buenas dias, amigo* — my name's Laredo. Juan Laredo."

Part Three

11

Blood on the Saddle

HE was born in the village of El Paso a few miles south of the Rio Grande. French blood flowed in his veins for his father, Etienne Danton, had been an officer in the army of France serving the Archduke Maximilian, the imposed Emperor of Mexico. When Etienne was killed defending the Archduke in the Mexican revolution, his lover, a peasant girl called Pilar Laredo, died of heartbreak shortly after giving birth to Juan. Reared by his grandmother, Juan grew into an attractive, carefree youth with swarthy good looks. In time his grandmother died and Juan saddled up and sought fresh fields north of the border.

He became a vaquero on several ranges

but was of so roaming a disposition that he quickly left each in turn, heading ever northwards, until one glorious but ill-fated day he reached the outskirts of Durward.

In no hurry to find a lodging-place, he meandered aimlessly along the banks of a river until he reached an idyllic backwater where tall pines silently contemplated their images in the still surface. Staking his horse on some high ground among the bush, he strolled towards the water's edge and spotting a shady rockpile decided to stretch out for a while. In its shallow basin, with sombrero tilted over his eyes, he soon drifted off to sleep. He neither saw nor heard the buggy approach.

For once Lucinda was alone, her faithful Maria busy with domestic chores. She stopped the buggy and sat gazing around herself. All was so still and tranquil. Over the translucent water dragonflies swooped and hovered, their tiny diaphanous wings reflecting the brilliant sunlight. Lucinda knew and loved this spot.

She got down from the buggy, smoothed down her dress and adjusted her sun-bonnet, then wended her way through rock and bush to gaze at the cool, tempting water. She had swum here often, but always while Maria kept watch.

Removing her bonnet and shaking free her ash-blonde hair, she continued looking at the water until all at once she made up her mind. She would go in.

She sank down by a rockpile and quickly disrobed. Carefully arranging her clothing she stood up as naked as the day she was born, feeling great satisfaction in being relieved of her garments, light though they were. The rock beneath her feet felt burning hot.

Gingerly she made her way towards the water and reaching the edge cautiously dipped her foot. It was deliciously cool, and she waded in up to her knees. She stood for several moments scooping up the water and bathing her thighs, stomach and bosom, and then, drawing a deep breath, she dived. Breaking the surface she struck out and in a few vigorous strokes reached the far side. For half an hour she darted about the water with the grace and agility of a fish, her slim white body clearly visible in the lucid water. Glowing with satisfaction, she eventually sought the shade of a rockpile and allowed the air to dry her nakedness. She yawned, stretched luxuriously, and lay back in surrender to the sultriness of the afternoon. Like Juan, hidden in the rocks not twenty yards distant, she was soon asleep.

The silence was broken by the impatient whinnying of Juan's horse and he sat up, knocking back his sombrero with the back of his hand. Where on earth was he? Ah yes, he remembered. Taking his eyes off the water, he glanced round — and froze.

The snake was inches from her head, poised and ready to strike, the cotton-white fangs starkly visible.

Laredo's hand dipped for his gun with lightning speed and in the next moment a white hot-slug had blasted the ugly head of the rocksnake sending it thrashing and writhing almost into the girl's lap. Lucinda's startled shrieks mingled with the frantic snorting of both horses, drowning the echo of Laredo's deadly shot. Racing over towards the girl, he grabbed the reptile's tail and hurled it into the water, where it sank slowly in hideous squirms. One glance told him that the girl was unharmed so he ran to calm each horse in turn then came back to her.

She lay on her side, her body covered with goose-pimples despite the intense heat. Her hand had closed instinctively over her dress but shock had overtaken her and she clung to the rock face in abject terror. Laredo fell to his knees beside her and took her in his arms. He was appalled by the iciness of her body. Cradling her head and crooning reassuringly into her ear, he felt her relax slowly and knew that the effects of the shock were beginning to subside.

He reached out with his foot and hooking more of her clothing managed to cover her exposed limbs. Only when he felt warmth flowing into her did he relax his hold on her. She gave a low moan and began to sob quietly, her whole body atremble. But he breathed easier. He knew that she would soon recover.

Presently she sat up and looked round in a sort of bewilderment, then memory crowded in on her and she shuddered. The filthy decapitated object wriggling and squirming beside her. God, she'd had a narrow escape.

Laredo squatted behind her in growing embarrassment. Overawed by her beauty, he had full view of her exquisite shape which as yet she had done nothing to conceal. In sitting up, she had dislodged most of her clothing and the small, firm, tip-tilted breasts protruded invitingly. He took his eyes from them with an effort and murmured: "Okay now."

She looked at him as though in a dream, shook her head, and said. "Goddam fool I am . . . saved my life . . . Sure are one hell of a shot."

Still she made no effort to dress. Just sat looking around her.

"Bathed here more times than I can remember and nothing like this has happened before," she went on. "Where in hell did you spring from?"

"Passing through. Saw the place and thought I'd take siesta. Didn't see you until my horse wakened me, then ... Name's Laredo. Juan Laredo."

"From Durward?" She casually pulled her clothes further on to her lap.

"El Paso, south of the border. Lovely place to swim. You often come here, eh? It's like the Garden of Eden."

"Yes," she said bitterly. "Even to the goddam snake. And now Eve wants to get dressed."

"Eve?"

She smiled at him, and her voice softened. "No — Lucinda. Haven't heard of me, have you? I'm one of the Coulters. When you get to Durward ask any of the townsfolk about us and you'll hear all kinds of stories, most of 'em bad."

"Of you, senorita? Then they are all liars in Durward."

He looked shocked, indignant. He also

looked strikingly handsome, even white teeth and olive skin, thick, wavy hair brushed straight back from a smooth brow. Typical Mexican, yet his eyes were piercingly blue.

"Thank you for that vote of confidence," said Lucinda, clutching her dress and getting to her feet. He turned round modestly and she grunted, "Bit late for that. Hope you liked what you saw. Well, best get a move on before they send out a search party. That's what comes of leaving Maria behind."

"Maria?"

"My servant. She always accompanies me on my outings, but couldn't make it today. Wait till she hears about this."

Lucinda quickly dressed herself then flashing him a winning smile said, "Thanks for everything, amigo, and adios."

His face fell.

"No, no," he protested. "I will see you home."

"Home!" She looked appalled. "Senor Laredo — if you knew what my father thinks of Mexicans . . . Guess you know how it is . . . "

He knew how it was all right. Gringo arrogance. Since leaving El Paso he'd met it in all shapes and forms and learned to live with it. He resented her assumption that he would understand but was so captivated by her he brushed it to one side as he accompanied her towards the buggy. She was swinging her sun-bonnet and looking demure yet her tone was sharp, assertive and above all confident. Obviously she was used to giving orders.

When she was perched on the buggy he looked up at her appealingly.

He said: "We can meet again?"

She kept silent, returning his gaze.

"Por favor," he insisted.

Those blue eyes were compelling. On sudden impulse, she replied quickly, "Yes."

His heart leapt. "Where? Here?"

"The day after tomorrow. Here at three. And Maria will be with me but no matter. She is discreet."

135

"I'll be here," he said fervently. "Waiting for you. I'll count the hours, the minutes, the seconds. Laredo will wait for you . . ."

She laughed lightly, cutting short his passionate outburst, and set the buggy in motion. "Thank you once more then. *Hasta luego,*" she cried.

Laredo watched until the buggy was out of sight then slowly made his way over to his horse, his mind in a whirl. He felt light, heady and completely unable to grasp the situation. Such incredible good fortune.

Siesta was over when he rode into Durward and the town was coming to life. He found himself a room at the 'Ace Saloon' and resigned himself to the interminable hours before he would see her again.

To eke out his dwindling money he played poker, and with such success that he was besieged by girls whose mercenary aims were stimulated by his physical charm. But he snubbed them all, thinking only of Lucinda.

Discreet enquiries around town confirmed her assertion that none would speak good of the Coulters. Jed Harker, the blacksmith, was the most forthcoming. His father had been in the same wagon-train that brought Adam Coulter, and he knew the family history well. Shots of rye, paid for by Laredo, loosened Jed's normally reticent tongue, and paid dividends, colourful though his account was.

Adam, the father, was a bastard. It was a pity the dogie that took him in the leg hadn't finished him off. Avoid him like the plague, though that was easy done, seeing as how he hardly left the ranch. Ben was as big a bastard as his father, only not near so smart, and Kit, Lucinda's twin brother, was as deep as a mountain lake. No womaniser, not like young Jess, always hanging around that no-good Nell James. Lucinda? Ah — a real beauty but not often seen in town. As remote and unattainable as a condor, prouder than a goddam peacock. The town wondered who she would get as a husband but whoever he was God help him.

Draining Harker of all information, Laredo felt he had known the Coulters all his life, and if he harboured apprehension of them, drowned it with thoughts of Lucinda. He, Juan Laredo, would capture the mountain condor.

12

ANXIOUSLY he waited for her in the silent glade and when he caught the sound of an approaching buggy his pulse raced.

At last she was here, radiant in flowing dress and flowered sun-bonnet. Even the sight of Maria by her side, eyeing him with overt curiosity tinged with admiration, could not suppress his elation.

"Lucinda!" he cried, sweeping off his sombrero.

She smiled at him.

"*Buenos dias, senor* — no snakes today?"

He threw back his head and laughed gleefully.

"All are afraid of Laredo, *no es verdad?*" He lightly patted his holsters and Maria sniggered at his histrionics, falling silent at Lucinda's frown.

Maria said hastily: "Think I'll walk

along the river bank."

What an attractive senorita, thought Laredo, flashing her an appreciative smile, and so thoughtful.

He didn't wait until Maria was out of sight but had helped Lucinda down from the buggy and taken her into his arms, murmuring endearments in her ear with all his pent-up Latin fervour. Resisting him with indulgent smiles, Lucinda took him by the hand and led him to the water's edge where they sat talking for an hour or more. Occasionally, she would permit a kiss but nothing more, and Laredo had to content himself with gazing into her lovely eyes. Time sped by and when they heard Maria returning Lucinda got to her feet and smoothed down her dress. "Time to be going."

Laredo's face registered dismay and she laughed, patting him on the cheek. "Don't look so sad, Juan: there's always tomorrow."

"*Si*," he said, giving an exaggerated sigh, "*Manana*. Laredo will be here, waiting for you. Always waiting for you."

"Ah! Here comes my faithful Maria. Now I really must go. Until tomorrow then, Juan."

So began the series of clandestine meetings with Lucinda ever tantalising and Laredo increasingly ardent. Her occasional haughtiness he dismissed, knowing her autocratic background, but he could scarcely contain his irritation at her persistent refusal to let him possess her.

Each successive meeting only added to his frustration but she would not yield in spite of his almost demented pleading.

I will not, she declared firmly, be taken in the field like some dogie.

Where then, thought Laredo wildly. Certainly not in the town and the ranch-house was out of the question.

It was stalemate — a position he would not, could not, accept. Knowing the delights beneath the dresses she wore drove him almost crazy with desire. He had to have her.

Then, one afternoon, she astonished him with her suggestion. The ranch-house. Her bedroom. She had thought it out carefully. He could come through the wood at the back of the house when it was dark. Maria would be waiting for him, guiding him with a lamp. They could trust Maria. She would do just as she was told.

Laredo was stunned. He just stared at her.

But she was adamant, almost pleading. Everything would be okay and just think of it, Juan — my own bedroom.

"But your father?" cried Laredo.

"No one will know, for God's sake. You've got to come, Juan. I will not be taken in the open . . . "

Laredo thought swiftly. The risk was enormous, but the prize ecstatic. He gave a brief nod of assent. "When?"

"Tonight," she said triumphantly, and launched into details of her plan.

When Durward was ablaze with light and in full swing Laredo stole quietly out of town and headed for the woods behind the Two Bar X. Tethering his roan to a tree trunk, he made his way towards the ranch-house with all the stealth of an Apache brave. Maria was waiting for him, guiding him with her oil lamp.

Reaching the back of the house, he slithered into the ante-room where she waited breathlessly. He said nothing but gripped her shoulder in appreciation, then went into Lucinda's room. Maria sank into a chair, sighing with relief. Shortly after, her cheeks began to burn. Try as she did she could not drown the rhythmic creaking of the bed next door.

Laredo spent most of the following day stretched out on his bed in the 'Ace Saloon', blowing smoke-rings at the ceiling and reliving the ecstasy of the night. Lucinda had transcended even his expectations and with such expert love-making that he still tingled at the memory of it.

At length his euphoric state subsided and he got up. From his window, he watched three men riding abreast down the street, proud and arrogant in the saddle.

The Coulter brothers.

There was no mistaking Kit. His resemblance to Lucinda was uncanny. Ben looked brutal and brooding. Jess's eyes, as ever, were bold and roving. Laredo wondered what they would have thought had they known of his affair with their sister.

It wasn't possible to visit the Two Bar X that night but the following night found him again creeping through the woods, again guided by Maria's lamp. Lucinda was waiting for him in the darkness of her room, pulsating with excitement. It was even better than the first time.

Then came the third and final time.

Maria had closed the door behind him and he slipped into Lucinda's eager, waiting arms, smothering her with kisses, when the other door burst open. In roared Ben Coulter like an enraged bull with Kit immediately behind, his yell drowning Lucinda's hollow cry of despair. Before Laredo could spring from the bed Ben's gun had thudded into his temple sending him flying against the wall. Through a red haze he saw Lucinda cowering wide-eyed among the pillows, her legs drawn up tightly. Before he slumped to the floor, Ben had him in his grip and was dragging him along a corridor and into the open where a high-standing buckboard stood waiting by a corral.

13

ASTRIDE his horse, Delaney warily eyed Laredo. His gun was pointing directly at the Mexican's heart and he raised it a fraction. His brain was racing. Why had they gunned down the posse? To claim the reward for themselves? What else? At least this greaseball with the blue eyes wouldn't get his hands on any of it. One false move and he'd blast him, even if his sidekicks immediately retaliated.

He growled: "One move and you're crow-bait. Savvy?"

Laredo raised his hands in mock horror.

"Put away your gun, Senor Delaney. I mean no harm. See — my guns are asleep in their holsters. Have I not just saved your life?" The tone was mild yet quietly authoritative.

"What's your angle, amigo?" demanded

Delaney suspiciously.

"Just that I want you. You are the best."

Delaney waited and Laredo went on calmly, "Followed your career from Mason City to San Felipe and you're good. Very good. The Overland was excellent. What went wrong? The senorita, I expect; always it is the senorita. But we should not hang around here talking. There are posses everywhere looking for you. *Vamos* — Let us go where we can talk in safety. This is Romero and this is Gomez. Come, my friend."

"Where you heading?"

"The Sierras, south of San José."

Delaney shrugged. Good as place as any, he supposed. But he still could not figure out the Mexican and why he had saved his hide.

"Okay — the Sierras."

They rode all day, stopping only at the occasional water-hole, and still Laredo didn't enlighten him as to his true intentions. Not that Delaney was bothered. The guy wasn't born who could push him around. Besides, he was brooding on the loss of the loot and what he would do to that woman when he caught up with her.

They came across Mort Jacoby that evening. With his twisted, broken neck and protruding tongue, he wasn't a pretty sight. A wind had got up and his swaying body made the branch creak. Delaney reckoned he'd been dead three days. Served him right. He wouldn't listen — none of them would. That was why they were all crow-bait and he was still riding. But the last job had been a near thing. Not his fault though — that goddam female. Mitch had been right.

Laredo looked impassively at the corpse but Romero and Gomez crossed themselves quickly and looked away. Romero, Laredo's trusted lieutenant and first recruit to his band, was particularly affected. Not so very long ago he would have been in the same position as Jacoby had it not been for Laredo. He owed his life to Laredo, and would help him fulfil his quest, but once it was over he was making for the border with his share of the wealth they would accumulate. To hell with this life with its long, hot days in the saddle and every man's hand turned against you. He would have a stucco-fronted hacienda and a hundred vaqueros, wine the finest in Mexico. And he would wear the finest outfit you ever saw. Highly polished riding-boots of finest leather and a set of Californian spurs which tinkled as he rode. A red silken shirt and striped cravat with gold stick-pin and soft leather holsters embossed in silver with the design of his hacienda. Senoritas? Ah yes — senoritas, black-haired beauties with sparkling eyes and full red lips. Burly moustachioed Gomez had no such thoughts but lived merely for the day. He was as easy-going as Romero was solemn until roused for no apparent reason, betraying the ferocity dormant in his volatile nature.

The party rode on with Laredo leading the way and Romero bringing up the rear with the posse's horses in tow. The wind had strengthened and an ominous cloud had piled up in the east. Birds were taking to the air and jack-rabbits, after startled looks, bolting for their holes. Laredo turned in the saddle and pointed to a line of high rock.

Reaching the sanctuary of the rocks, they lost no time in bedding down the horses, taking a pull at their canteens and covering their faces with their sweat-rags. Then they waited.

The wind was now howling over the landscape, tearing frenziedly at the giant cacti and uprooting tumbleweed to send it rolling crazily over the gouged, jagged earth. Day turned into night as the dust blotted out the sun and came roaring ferociously over the countryside, burying everything in its choking path. The din was appalling, and the men hunched themselves deeper into the rock face, cursing behind their sweat-rags. At length the wind began to drop and as quickly as it had started the dust-storm subsided. A heavenly silence was beginning to settle over the landscape.

Shaking themselves free of dust, the

outlaws emerged from their sanctuary almost unrecognisable, and immediately saw to the horses. Two had perished. After watering the rest from their canteens, they lost no time in resuming their journey, hoping for some mountain stream. Three weary hours were to pass, however, before they came across one, by which time they were well into the Sierras where mountain-sides loomed white and shining one moment and in the next dark, menacing and treacherous. Darkness was closing round them as they took their fill of water after which, worn out by the storm, they unstrapped their blanket-rolls and bedded down for the night.

Before moving off next morning, shortly after sun-up when it was warm, they stripped off and doused themselves in the clear mountain stream, ridding themselves of dust. Laredo, to Delaney's cynical amusement, was the last to enter the water and with some reluctance. When the Mexican turned his back on him Delaney's eyes widened in astonishment. "Christ Almighty!" he shouted.

Laredo swung round, naked hatred in his face.

"Now you know why I want you," he said.

Laredo made no further mention of his scarred back until noon that day when they again broke their journey. Romero and Gomez were snoozing and out of earshot but in any case knew their leader's story, or what he had chosen to reveal of it.

He glanced at Delaney who lay on his back with his head nestling in his enlaced fingers, hat over his face, shading himself from the sun.

"Know Durward?" Laredo's tone was sharp, incisive.

Delaney sat up slowly.

"Passed through. Good range country."

Laredo said: "Yes — and most of it owned by the Coulter family. Heard of them?"

"Nope."

"The Two Bar X. Biggest hacienda in the territory. Peon labour. There's

Adam Coulter and his three sons, Ben, Kit and Jess. Powerful people. And they have a ramrod called Jackson — Slim Jackson."

Laredo's face was flint-hard.

"So?" said Delaney, although he guessed what was coming.

"I want them killed. All of them."

Delaney took time to light a cheroot, then nodded at the Mexican, "They did that to you?"

"Yes."

"Nice people. The finger too?"

Laredo glanced at his mutilated hand. "No. An accident when I was a *muchacho*."

"So you want them planted — that figures. But why me, Laredo? You've got Romero and Gomez. Where do I come in?"

"And two others besides. Five of us in all and you make six. It will need six for what I have in mind. But I am not a *bandito*, Delaney. Finish what I have to do and then I will return to my own country."

Delaney knew better than to ask why Laredo had been savagely whipped but, remembering his talk about senoritas, suspected that some woman was at the bottom of it. Instead he said. "What do we do for dinero in the meanwhile? Guy's got to live."

"No cause for concern," was Laredo's puzzling reply.

He did not elaborate so Delaney, nodding towards the posse's horses, said, "Leastways we can get a buck or two on that lot. Know an old sourdough in the hills who'd like to get his hands on them. Indian Sam. Heard of him?"

Laredo shrugged.

"No — but if you can do a deal, why not?"

"These plans of yours. What's in them for Delaney?"

"Big reward. Better than the Overland, and when it's all over, you are free to leave."

Delaney whistled softly.

"Better than the Overland, eh? Count me in, amigo. When do we start?"

"Tomorrow — after we have rested."

"Where?"

"San José."

"San José? Why not Durward?"

"The Coulters keep a great deal of their money in the bank at San José. Durward has no marshal."

"Sure know a lot about these Coulters, Laredo."

"When you set out to kill a mountain lion, you first get to know its habits. You know that, Delaney — which is why I want you."

Delaney nodded. "That figures."

Laredo smiled thinly, then relapsed into a moody silence. Talk of the Coulters had revived bitter memories and once again the smouldering fires within him were beginning to flare. When he had finished with the Coulters and Jackson it would be the turn of the bitch Maria, the one who had betrayed him and Lucinda.

Lucinda — the most agonising memory of all.

He lay back against the rock face,

trying to keep himself in check. Delaney was new to this mood but Romero and Gomez knew it only too well and left him severely alone. Delaney did not question him further but wondered why he should begin his vendetta by robbing the Coulters of some of their gold instead of going for them. Still, that was okay by him. He had no quarrel with the Coulters, and gold was gold.

They reached Laredo's hide-out at nightfall, another almost inaccessible cavern high in the mountains, but infinitely superior to the last one Delaney had taken refuge in. The Mexicans had gone to great lengths to ensure comfort, nonetheless Delaney yearned for the bustle of town life with its saloons, poker and dance-hall girls.

Tomas and Pedro, the two who had been left behind, greeted them effusively, but eyed Delaney with apprehension. Not only was he a gringo but well-known as a *bandito* with an evil reputation.

Galloping towards the small town of

Hansen's Drift, Emma's first thoughts were to put as much distance between Delaney and herself as possible, then, when practicable, to rid herself of the weighty bullion, which she had taken only to deprive him of it. The dollar bills she would keep but the bullion was a deep source of worry.

First she didn't know what to do with it and second it was so bulky it could draw unwarranted attention. And that petrified her. Once she had seen a woman hanged for robbery, and the memory haunted her. How the woman had pleaded with her executioners to be swung low enough so that witnesses would be discouraged from looking up her dress as she dangled. But compliance with the request had incurred virtual strangulation, and Emma shuddered at the thought.

At the first opportunity she reined in, dragged the heavy saddlebags to a cliff edge and sent them hurtling. Before the echoes of their fall had faded in the ravine she was in the saddle again and racing towards the town where she planned to hole up for a few days then take the stage to Mason City to begin life anew.

Conflicting emotions were tearing her apart.

Rachel's murder didn't merit a single thought but losing Delaney was devastating, even though she had brought it on herself. She missed him sorely yet hoped that the posse had caught up with him for with Delaney alive she knew that she could never again have peace of mind. She would always be looking over her shoulder.

Hansen's Drift was a one-horse burg but anything was better than the cabin at San Felipe. During her brief stay, Emma made herself as inconspicuous as possible, then, when she felt that the time was ripe, set off for Mason City.

14

THE tattered curling poster on the wall of the saloon proclaiming that a substantial reward would be paid by the Mesa City firm of Cole and Hargreaves to anyone with information leading to the arrest of the robbers of the Overland Stage went unheeded by Delaney as he sat drinking his beer and studying the bank opposite through the saloon's fly-blown windows. When every external feature was imprinted on his mind he finished his drink and strolled over and went into the bank. Making tentative enquiries at the counter, he noted the interior: three cashiers behind the high wooden counter with guns within easy reach and the safe in the left-hand corner.

Satisfied by what he had seen, Delaney stepped out into the sunlight and retraced his steps to the saloon. Freeing his horse from the hitching-rail, he swung himself up into the saddle and set off at a jog-trot along the broad street. San José was quiet at this time of day.

At the southern end of the street where clustered a miscellany of wooden storehouses, his alert eyes fastened on whiskey barrels strategically placed at the entrance of each storehouse and his face twitched into a half smile. On he rode, out into the plain and on towards the distant peaks where Laredo and his men waited.

Arrogance was a habit with Delaney but if the Mexicans resented it they did not show it. He outlined his plan for robbing the bank with all the authority of one used to giving orders and so enthusiastic was the band that even Laredo nodded his head in approval. Delaney was the cynosure of all eyes and enjoyed every moment of it.

Fire!
Panic gripped the trail-town of San José like a living thing, throwing open

doors and windows and blanching the faces of its citizens. Out they poured into the streets and alleyways drawn as if by a magnet to the southern end of Main Street where livid tongues of flame engulfed the storehouses, roaring and crackling defiance. The crowd surged down the street like a tidal wave carrying all before it save one rock-like figure — Delaney, astride a stallion, serene of eye and coldly taking in the scene.

Everything was going splendidly.

The storehouses were a mass of flame and threatening to spread. Horror-stricken eyes were looking in vain for water. Only black patches of damp could be seen at the bottom of each emptied whiskey barrel and where water had seeped through the boards of the sidewalk.

Romero and Tomas, now waiting excitedly at the other end of the town, had done their work well. Earlier in the day, they had driven nails deep into each barrel, withdrawing them at the appropriate time.

With the word 'fire' ringing in their ears, people had deserted the bank and only the shirt-sleeved cashiers hovered round the open doorway, caught between apprehension and the call of duty. Delaney, strategically mounted opposite and with well-oiled sixshooters free in his holsters, caught sight of Laredo and Gomez emerging from a shady alleyway. Across the street they raced, shouldering aside the astonished cashiers and into the bank.

Delaney's guns leapt into his hands, spitting lead at the bank men and sending them reeling into the street. Endless minutes, then out of the bank dashed Laredo and Gomez, clutching sacks and stooping curiously as though expecting a hail of bullets. Balding Pedro, afire with impatience, was waiting for them with their horses.

It was all so smoothly done, so incredibly easy, that Delaney almost laughed aloud. He waited until Laredo and Gomez were mounted then turned in the saddle for a final glance at the red glow at the end of the street. Casually he wondered if there had been shooting inside of the bank. Certainly he had heard none but maybe his own shots had drowned the noise. Reaching the far end of town, he broke into a gallop and soon caught up with the trio going hell for leather for the mountains. Romero and Tomas were to join up with them later.

A red haze hung over San José as its citizens, heedless of the now discovered bank raid, fought desperately for its very existence.

Although regretting the necessity of gunning down the bank men, Laredo was elated by the success of the raid, confirming the wisdom of his decision to enlist Delaney, whose meticulous attention to detail had again paid off.

Laredo's initial thrust against the Coulters had triumphed and in a way which would infuriate old Adam, but would it draw any of them from their stronghold, making them more vulnerable? He hoped so. Let any of them come searching the mountains and he would be waiting. When his next thrust was put into operation, it would begin to dawn on the Coulters who was behind it all.

Half his face was in shadow but the visible part showed a tired, lazy grin and drooping eyelids. He was stretched out on a makeshift bed in the entrance to the cavern and the slanting rays of the dying sun were picking out the curling hairs on his exposed chest and forearms. Delaney, in satisfied mood, was taking it easy.

The Mexicans were celebrating with raw, native whiskey and then Tomas picked up his guitar and began strumming an old Castilian air, filling the cavern with the sound of haunting music. The rest joined in, humming in unison, until Delaney stirred and sat up.

"Hi — Chico!" Tomas looked across at him.

"Ees Tomas — not Chico."

"Whatever your goddam name is, quit making that row."

Tomas looked round his friends, shrugged, and carried on playing.

Delaney bawled: "Don't listen, do you, spic? I said shut that now. You want to wake the whole territory?"

Tomas stopped playing and in the dying echoes Delaney heard them muttering. Romero, bottle in hand, got unsteadily to his feet and looked down at the outlaw. "Why you not happy, gringo?"

Delaney never took chances, which is why he had stayed alive, and even in this bleak, remote spot he wasn't taking any.

Snarled Delaney: "Why doesn't he take a goddam bugle and let everybody know where we're holed up?"

"The senor is right, Romero." Laredo stood in the entrance to the cavern. "We must not take chances. Come, amigo — let us rest now. We have work tomorrow."

Laredo's tone was calm, soothing. Taking Romero gently by the arm, he led him to the other side of the cavern and set him down. Romero continued to glare at Delaney, muttering darkly to himself.

Laredo ran his eye over the rest of his band. "Sleep now, amigos: we have celebrated enough." He looked at Delaney. "You too, I think, senor. I will continue to keep watch."

For a moment it looked as though Delaney was about to retort but thinking better of it he merely shrugged and settled down. Laredo contained his relief. The sooner this business with the Coulters was over the better, he told himself. Delaney and his band were a dangerous mixture.

The following day Laredo again led his men down from the mountains in a second bid to harass the Coulters. This time the destination was a dozen or so miles north of Durward, a ford in the fast-flowing river where rocks abounded on either side providing excellent protection.

Delaney was wary. Even the frontier towns must be alarmed by the wave of banditry — the scalping of the troopers, the Overland Stage hold-up and now the burning of San José. Posses would be more vigilant than ever.

Reaching the ford, the band fanned out, taking cover behind rock and boulder. They had not long to wait. Dust on the horizon signalled the approach of the cattle drive.

The herd, comprising both long and shorthorns all branded with the distinctive Two Bar X brand, was not large by normal standards, and was destined for the railway cattle-yards at Mason City. Riding point and almost invisible in the cloud of dust was a peon vaquero. Laredo had given strict orders to his band not to gun down any peon. The Mexicans would obey, but the was not certain of Delaney who took a delight in killing for its own sake. He didn't expect any gringos to be in the drive but any that were could be shot. Stampeding Coulter cattle was just another way to nettle them and hopefully, like the bank raid, draw them from their ranch.

Familiar with cattle drives, the waiting band knew what to expect. Cattle hated water, so first a string of mustangs would be led across the ford to encourage them by their example, then the herd would be split in two divisions with a vaquero to coax each one into the stream.

The band held fire until the mustangs and most of the first division were over then opened up with a deadly fusillade scattering them in all directions. Those caught in mid-stream panicked most and several of them, bellowing and snorting, were swept away to drown in the treacherous undercurrents.

The din was deafening as beasts bucked, reared and stumbled to their knees, crashed into by others equally terrified. Dust rose more than ever, thick, choking clouds of it which had the men reaching for their sweat-rags. Then, through one such swirl, Laredo spotted Ben Coulter and a thrill shot along the length of his nerves.

Ben was mounted and on the far side

of the ford, doing his utmost to control the stampede.

Laredo fired quickly and for a split second saw Ben slump in the saddle before dust once more engulfed him. Laredo kept peering into the clouds of dust hoping to confirm that he had indeed hit Ben but it was no use. He had disappeared from view. Delaney thumped his back. "Let's go to hell out of here."

Laredo could not complain. Delaney was only following orders. Scatter the herd, shoot as many as possible, and back to the hide-out. A lingering look and he was on his feet, racing after the outlaw.

Living in the open had palled on Delaney and his brief excursion into San José had whetted his appetite for town life. Bluntly he told Laredo that he was riding into Durward that night. The risk, he maintained, was minimal. No names had appeared on the 'wanted' posters for the Overland robbery and it was highly unlikely that Emma Carson would have told anyone, not wanting to implicate herself in the robbery. Delaney knew exactly what she had done. Set the posse after him, then disappeared with the loot.

Laredo hesitated when told of his intention, but only for a moment. Tension in the cavern had increased, and it might not be a bad thing to see the back of Delaney, even for a short while. Laredo knew that he would return. His promise of high reward was too tempting for Delaney and whatever feelings they had for one another Delaney trusted him.

The 'Silver Dollar' was in full swing. Poker players with foaming pints at their elbows clustered round the small tables while a droopy-eyed cowhand with a smoke dangling from the corner of his mouth provided the music on a bullet-pitted piano. Girls, short on talent but long on lust, were pirouetting on the stage at the far end of the saloon, barely visible in the blue haze of smoke. The room fairly hummed until a redhaired woman in a scarlet dress burst on to the stage to a fanfare from the pianist. The dancers scattered as all eyes turned on the woman. An ear-splitting yell went up from the crowd.

Arkansas Amy!

When the noise subsided, she wriggled her powdered shoulders, making her creamy exposed bust do impossible things, then stopped dramatically:

"Howdy, boys?"

More stamping and clapping until she waved it into silence. Throwing back her head she asked: "How's about the dress, fellers? Becoming, huh? Becoming off soon."

Another burst of cheering.

"Calls it my barbed-wire dress. Protects the property but don't hide the view none." When the laughter died, she looked across at the pianist.

"Okay Bill — your favourite and my favourite."

Her voice was coarse, husky, yet somehow appealing, and the crowd loved it. She sang another two numbers, did even more impossible things with her bust, then went off to rapturous applause.

Delaney turned back to his beer, as appreciative as any in the crowd. He took a long pull at it. He could still feel the dust from the stampede at the back of his throat.

Casually he wondered if Mitch had teamed up again with the Galtons, and if they were in town. But he didn't intend to ask the creep behind the bar. Charlie, or whatever his name was, was too goddam big for his boots; wanted cutting down to size. That quip he had made when first he had asked for a drink. Popskull or tarantula-juice, the cheeky bastard had replied. He had not wanted to draw attention to himself or the bar-keep would now be so filled with lead he would fall through the bottom of his coffin. Nobody joked with Delaney, least of all a squidgy-noised bar-keep.

"Whiskey," a deep voice at his side ordered.

Charlie swung round in some surprise.

"Sure, Mr Coulter."

Coulter!

Delaney's eyes flicked sideways. A good-looking hombre with clean-cut features. A Coulter, eh? But which one? Delaney lit a quirly and watched him take his drink over to one of the tables. There was some talk then a chair was found for him and he joined in the card game.

Delaney turned back to the bar-keep.

Casually he said: "Know that guy from somewhere."

Charlie snorted. "Who doesn't? Thought everyone knew Kit Coulter. Folk reckon he's better than Ben or Jess but me I ain't so sure. All Coulters is bad medicine."

Delaney lost interest. He straightened, polished off his drink and looked round. The noise in the saloon was getting to him so he wandered to the batwings. Breathing deeply of the night air, he suddenly made up his mind. He found what he was looking for at the other end of town, an hour of passion in the arms of some filly by the name of Nell James. She

173

was an accomplished performer and he was well satisfied by the time he emerged from the bordello.

It was dark outside but there was sufficient light from the brothel windows to see across the street. Freeing his horse, Delaney was about to mount when a pair of riders drew abreast of him — Kit Coulter and an hombre who looked more greaser than gringo.

Delaney had no quarrel with the Coulters, but the sooner Laredo finished with them, the sooner he could quit and head north.

Crouching behind his saddle, he felt for his knife, sliding it part way up the sheath. His hand closed more firmly over the hilt. He held his breath then suddenly threw, at the same time leaping into the saddle and bringing down his spurs. Flinging a backwards glance, he cursed to see that Kit still held his horse but it must have been a near thing. Laredo hadn't been certain if he had shot Ben and now here his brother Kit surviving by a hair's breadth. Rich hombres, the Coulters, and with more luck than they deserved.

Delaney rode on, scattering drunks in all directions in his haste to make the mountains. The following day a bounty hunter by the name of Cade Forster booked in at the 'Silver Dollar' saloon, enquiring about a gunslinger with a scarred face called Joe Mitchell.

15

IN far-off Hansen's Drift Emma Carson waited patiently outside the saloon for the stagecoach which was to take her to Mason City, a town she had never seen but knew to be an oasis of civilisation in this wild, lawless land. It was at least a day's ride, across plain and semi-desert.

She had dispensed with her deliberate dowdiness of the past few days and although still inconspicuously dressed appeared neat and demure in sun-bonnet and calico frock. Not wanting to attract undue attention, she kept her head lowered and curls tucked out of sight, nonetheless a couple of locals with time on their hands were beginning to eye her with mounting interest. By her feet stood a small, sturdy chest containing all her possessions including the dollar bills, her passport to happiness. As the locals ogled her more overtly, her patience ran out and she kept looking up and down the sun-splashed street for the stage. Then, just as one of the locals plucked up courage and was about to speak, the stage appeared at the top of the street in a flurry of dust. Emma let out a sigh of relief.

Driver and shotgun were in a hurry to reach Mason by nightfall, eager to snatch a few hours' entertainment before moving on to Mesa, and gruffly demanded that she get a move on. Seething with indignation, Emma hissed, "Then help me with this goddam chest."

"Allow me, ma'am," said a voice from inside the coach, then a head was poked through the window. "Phineas Thorneloe at your service."

Emma stared.

Phineas Thorneloe? Nobody could be called that. Must be some sort of preacher man or maybe a medicine drummer, a quack-doctor hawking his quack medicines from town to town. Still, whatever he was, he moved with alacrity.

First her chest was slung into the stage then she was given a helping hand. Holding her frock at the hip, she stepped inside and saw that there was another occupant, an elderly man in sombre broadcloth who looked like a legal gent or a banker. He gave her a sickly grin of acknowledgement, then sank back again in his corner seat. Phineas planted himself beside her and instinctively her hand went out to the chest at her side.

The stagecoach jerked into life and went rumbling down the rutted road and into the plain.

She gave Phineas a sidelong glance. The nose was long and thin and he had a mop of unruly hair which kept falling into a pair of close-set eyes which had the suspicion of a squint. His dress was equally bizarre: a red and white checked shirt, black cravat, and a vest with a sheen of crushed blackberries.

"Yes, ma'am, the name is Thorneloe — Phineas Thorneloe. My profession, a doctor of medicine. My speciality is Abraham Harcourt's magic elixir. You haven't heard of it? Guaranteed to make you feel ten years younger after one bottle. Not, I hasten to add, that *you* need any of it." He paused, allowing time for the compliment to sink in, then, "Mason City your destination?"

Emma gave the barest nod, hoping he would take the hint and stop babbling.

"Mine too," he went on in his high-pitched voice. "A fine city, I hear. Will you be staying long?"

"Yes, I suppose so," she answered uncertainly.

She turned her head and looked out of the window. Mile after mile of rolling grassland, as uninteresting as Mr Thorneloe's talk.

He gave a snigger. "You don't sound sure, but that of course is the prerogative of a young lady. Not to be sure about anything. And why not, indeed? The world is too full of folk all so certain of themselves. I — er — didn't catch your name."

Emma turned again and gave him a vacant stare.

"Your name. I didn't catch your name."

"Oh! It's Em . . . "

"Em?"

"Er — Mina." Was there no way to shut this guy up. What would Delaney have made of him? Delaney. Suddenly she felt a great sadness.

The medicine drummer was still prattling on. What was her surname? Where would she stay in Mason City? Did she know anyone there? She replied in monosyllables, growing curter with each one. She even wished the old guy opposite would waken up to stem the flow of talk but he dozed on, head lolling on his chest.

If Thorneloe's chatter did not give way at least the plain did and now the stage was bumping and rattling its way through gorge and valley. Emma feigned sleep, the only course open to her to avoid the medicine drummer's talk, then, in a short while, didn't need to. The sway of the coach had lulled her into a merciful oblivion.

It was the simultaneous crack of rifle

shot and sudden screech of the brakes which jolted Emma out of her sleep and her immediate reaction was to throw a protective arm over the chest at her side. Dry-gulched, b'God. The old man opposite was sitting bolt upright, eyes starting from his head but Phineas Thorneloe had his poked out of the window. "Road's blocked," he squeaked.

Emma didn't need to be told. Delaney and Mitch had often used the same tactics. Rocks and maybe a tree trunk.

"Down you fool," she cried, grabbing Phineas by the coat tail. Another bullet smacked into the woodwork and he was down on the floor with Emma. Two more slugs whistled into the coach and she looked up at the old man. There was no point in telling him to get down. He'd fallen sideways on the seat, blood trickling from his forehead. Grovelling on the floor with Phineas, she listened to the exchange of fire. The thought of being robbed and arriving penniless in Mason was making her ill. Phineas, more realistically, was thinking of his life.

The stage had ground to a halt and there was a sudden fearful silence. Sensing that the driver and shotgun had perished, Phineas broke into a cold sweat, and Emma, huddled beside him, felt his whole frame beginning to tremble. Both held their breath, listening to the ominous approach of horses' hooves. The clip-clop stopped, then came the footsteps. In the next moment the stagecoach door was flung open and the pair were looking up the barrel of a pointing rifle.

"D-don't shoot . . . please . . . " Phineas now kept his eyes tightly shut. A dark stain was spreading slowly between his legs. Emma was now looking beyond the barrel — a Mexican, and she knew what that meant. Scrambling to her feet, she sank back on the hard, wooden seat, waiting. The bandit still held his peace, waiting no doubt for his companions. Presently they rode up on the other side of the coach, two of them, and liberally armed. Dismounting, one of them went to the back of the stage to haul down the trunk belonging to the old man, while the other, ignoring Phineas and Emma, searched the inside of the coach.

No one spoke and the silence was eerie.

The medicine drummer's carpet-bag containing his assortment of quackery was put alongside the old man's trunk, then the searcher turned to Emma's chest. Her eyes were wide with apprehension. He reached for it and her hand shot out. "No jewellery — only clothes."

The bandit stared at her then, taking hold of the chest, gave it to the other, who placed it beside the rest of the baggage. First to be opened was Thorneloe's bag and the contents were unceremoniously dumped on the hard ground, then the locks were shot off the old man's trunk. Foisty legal documents joined the broken bottles of patent medicines until a hiss of triumph announced the discovery of tiny sacks of gold-dust. These were quickly transferred to the saddlebags of the horses. Then it was the turn of Emma's chest. The locks were shot off, the lid flung open and, as the girl had said, only clothing was to be seen. Dresses, blouses and skirts were hauled out in disgust and thrown to the wind. A few dollar bills escaped their caches to swirl aimlessly but insufficient to draw the attention of the bandits. Which senorita travelling by stagecoach did not sew some bills into her clothing? The old man's gold watch was added to the loot but altogether it had not been an exciting haul. Disappointed, the leader looked at Phineas, prone on the floor. He nodded across at the third bandit, still covering the pair. He grinned then prodded the medicine drummer.

Convinced his end was near, Phineas stumbled from the stagecoach, blinking in the stark light. His face was chalk white. To his left sprawled the body of the driver and to his right that of the shotgun. On the skyline hovered the bald-headed harbingers of death, gathering for their grisly meal once the humans had departed.

The leader was smiling at him, a thin, cruel smile, and holding towards him one of his bottles. "Drink, amigo."

Phineas stared uncertainly.

"Drink."

Emma risked taking her eyes off the gun and glanced out of the window. She saw the bandit leader, hand on hip, legs braced back and holding out a bottle to Phineas who stood swaying in the breeze. The medicine drummer being made to taste his own wares. But there was nothing funny in it. Humour was unknown to this walrus-moustached Mexican. Beyond them she glimpsed items of her clothing, some clinging to bush or cacti but most being carried away in the capricious wind.

She watched while Phineas drank one bottle of his elixir under the cold gaze of the leader, then a second and then a third. Well aware of the contents, Phineas was growing more and more agitated. His stomach was beginning to heave and to the delight of the fascinated bandits he was making obscene noises from gut and bowel. Emma was appalled but couldn't look away. Now the medicine drummer was drinking his sixth bottle, holding his midriff, squirming and imploring the bandit with his eyes to let him stop. Unable to contain their delight longer, the bandits burst out laughing and Emma longed to cry out in protest. After the seventh bottle Phineas slumped to his knees, vomit and saliva drooling unchecked down his quivering chin. Wearied by the spectacle, the leader took his foot and sent him sprawling. Groaning and whimpering, Phineas crawled towards some straggling bush pursued by a horde of buzzing flies. The leader turned his attention to the stagecoach and Emma paled. She had known her fate from the outset but now that the moment had come she began to tremble. Resistance, she knew, was useless, but would compliance gain any advantage? Would they let her live — after?

Ordered from the stage, Emma gathered her frock about herself and, stepping into the sunlight, saw the bodies and Phineas, rolling in agony in the bush. The breeze lifted her hair about the nape of her neck and blew dust into her face. Knuckling it from her eyes, she met the bold, insolent stare of the leader. They stood in silence, looking at each other, until he waved towards a smooth slab of rock. She hesitated, but only for a moment, then walked over to it. She sank down, gave him an uncertain look, and laid back. The sky was a canopy of blue and she could feel the heat of the rock forcing its way through the back of her dress. Hearing his approach she closed her eyes, tugged free her dress and slowly lifted it. He stood above her, darkening her with his shadow. Gritting her teeth and throwing her head to one side, she thought hurry up and get it over, you oily bastard.

He came down on her all right but not the way he intended. The slug, striking him squarely between the shoulder-blades, pitched him headlong over her and he lay twisting and writhing in his death agonies. She pushed him off, sat up and watched him in wonder. Blood was trickling from his mouth and his exposed buttocks twitching with muscular spasms. There were more shots and she looked around wildly. One of the bandits was doing a macabre dance of death whilst the other was crawling with splintered jaw towards the stage.

What in hell was going on?

She froze against the rock, waiting and wondering.

Then he appeared along the side of the gorge, his high-standing bay picking its way through the shale. When he drew nearer she thought, thank God — an American.

He reined in, glanced at the Mexican squirming by the stage and pumped more slugs into him. A cursory look told him that the other two were dead. He sat still, looked at Emma, the bodies of the stage-driver and his shotgun, then towards Phineas moaning in the bush. The litter of documents and medicine bottles told him all.

Shoving his rifle back into the scabbard, he quickly dismounted, tied his horse to the stagecoach wheel, and to Emma's surprise, went scouring the bush. Kneeling by a clump of juniper he plucked some shrub then shouted over his shoulder, "Quick, woman — boil some water."

Emma was on her feet in a flash and hurrying towards the stage. While she was kindling a fire and setting on a pot to boil the stranger was letting loose a few shots, frightening the more audacious of the buzzards.

He came over to her and handed over the shrub he had collected. "When the water boils, put this in and let it simmer five minutes. I'll go see how he's doing. You okay?"

"Some," she said.

He nodded and set off towards the medicine drummer. She didn't envy him. She could smell the stink from where she squatted. The water was soon boiling and in went the shrub, turning it into a greenish colour. She looked up and saw the stranger coming across to her with Phineas in his arms. Laying him down in the shade of the stage, he went for his blanket-roll and canteen of water. Phineas, deathly white, made no sound as the blanket-roll was gently placed under his head. The stink was appalling and the stranger had his work cut out brushing aside the swarm of flies. A hastily-lit quirly helped dispel some of it. Ignoring Emma, Phineas's pants were hauled down and his lower body and limbs thoroughly washed, then the pants were cast into the bush.

Emma poured some of the liquid into a tin mug and brought it over. "This okay?"

He looked at it and nodded. "Get some pants off one of those guys. This one needs a new pair."

Emma shook her head in bewilderment but without protest selected the stage-driver and set about the distasteful task. Bearing the pants over her arm, she returned to the pair. Phineas was sitting up with lack-lustre eyes and the stranger was looking anxiously at the thin, drawn face. Liquid had dribbled from his mouth to stain the front of his checked shirt.

"Will he live?" she asked.

"The next hour will tell. Seen guys worse but that shrub always pulled them through. Learned it from the Hopi. Not much those Indians don't know about medicine. Toothache? Cure it in a minute with *is yerba del pasmo,* another of their shrubs. This guy a relation?"

"No. He was on the stage at Hansen's Drift. Never seen him before. He's a medicine drummer, would you believe? There was another guy, a legal gent I figure, but he was killed."

"Making for Mason City?"

"Was, but no chance now, not with that lot blocking the way. Guess it will have to be Mesa. Name's Mina Harper. What's yours?"

"Cade Forster."

"What do you do for a living, Mr Forster? Besides rescuing stage passengers, that is?"

"Collect boots and saddles."

Emma gave him a sharp look. Memory

pricked her but to no avail.

"Bounty hunter, eh?"

"Yes ma'am. Come on, let's get him into the stage. Sooner we make Mesa, sooner he sees a doctor."

"You'll drive?"

Cade looked around ruefully. "Can you suggest anyone else?"

"Reckon not," sighed Emma then, more softly. "Sure glad you moseyed, along. As God made little apples certain-sure we'd all be buzzard-meat by now. Goddam greasers."

Having made Phineas as comfortable as possible inside the stage, Cade strung out the horses behind then unbuckled the bandits' saddlebags and hauled out the tiny sacks of gold-dust. Emma, furtively glancing at what was left of her clothing, held her breath.

"Who owned this lot?" Cade held up a couple of sacks.

Emma gulped, but realising there was no fooling him said with a sigh, "The old man, I guess. Mine's all gone. Had it all sewn up in my clothes, then damn it if the greaseballs don't throw them to the wind. What do you aim to do with that lot?"

"Sure it all belonged to the old man? What about the drummer?"

"Phineas? Wouldn't have one nickel to rub up against another. No — that's the old man's I reckon, but I have no idea who he was or where he came from, and I guess the driver ain't going to tell us. Well, what do we do about it?"

"Talk to the drummer when he wakes up. He may know. Well, let's get moving. Getting inside or on top with me?"

"With you, with you. Couldn't stand the guy when he was normal, much less now. That garbage he sells: told me one bottle makes you feel ten years younger. The amount he's drunk, he'll be in diapers for the rest of his life."

The pair climbed up into the driving-seat and after some difficulty managed to turn round the stage and head back along the rock-strewn path, leaving behind the bleak scene of crumpled corpses and gathering flocks of scavengers.

Exhausted by her ordeal, Emma spoke little, but her mind was active. Mesa evoked bittersweet memories and she was depressed by the thoughts of returning there, however temporary her stay. And how was she going to manage without money? Somehow she couldn't see this bounty hunter sharing out the old man's gold-dust.

Bounty hunter.

Suddenly she remembered. Indian Sam's shack when she had been half asleep. A bounty hunter by the name of Cade Forster — after Joe Mitchell's scalp. She wished him luck but felt uneasy in his company. Bounty hunters tended to be on the side of the law. The law! The marshal at Mesa, Rowntree or whatever they called him, was he still after the Overland robbers? Folk reckoned he never let go of anything once he got his teeth into it. No, Mesa was a dismal prospect, and the sooner she got to hell out of it the better. Her thoughts raced on, growing more depressed with every turn of the wheels.

Cade, a quiet man, appreciated her silence, if not the cause of it. Handling the horses with skill he drove across the plain, thinking mainly of a scar-faced gunslinger operating somewhere round San José or Durward according to his last information.

Phineas survived the journey, thanks largely to Cade's remedy, but the moment they hit town he turned him over to the first doctor he could find, paying for his treatment out of his own pocket. Before leaving the grateful medicine drummer, he learned that the legal gent had been called Simon Blackwood and he came from some town up north by the name of Philipville. Money? He had no money: if there was any to be found in the coach it must belong to Blackwood or the young lady, most likely Blackwood.

Cade's next call was the office of the stagecoach line in Mesa where he handed over the bullet-riddled coach to a pair of astonished clerks. Penniless Emma was at his side, confirming all that he had said. When the coach had been taken

195

into custody, Cade held out his hand. Salvage money was a recognised reward and the clerks didn't argue. It was an appreciable amount.

Outside the office Cade ran his eye over the girl. Bedraggled, travel-stained, she looked utterly forlorn. He looked at his leather bag, sighed, and self-consciously pushed it into her hand. "Try the 'Golden Nugget' over there. Leastways the liquor's good."

The last she saw of him was riding his bay out of town. More than ever she wished him luck in his quest for Mitchell.

The 'Golden Nugget'? Not goddam likely. She couldn't live with the ghost of Delaney.

She wandered along the sidewalk, clutching her bag and drawing inquisitive stares, until she came to another hotel, the 'Alhambra'. Looked okay for one night. Tomorrow she would be on her way to Mason. She went up to the counter and the clerk looked up, then a hearty voice boomed out, "By the great horned toad — Emma Carson!"

Emma swung round.

Nell James, an old friend before she met Delaney, and at her side a suave-looking hombre with oily hair and long sideburns. Looked either a card-sharper or a brothel-keeper. He was in fact Jake La Rue, and the moment he set eyes on Emma, travel-stained though she was, he knew he had another employee.

Emma did not leave for Mason City the next day. She left for Durward in the same stagecoach as Nell and Jake.

16

MEANWHILE, in his mountain retreat, Laredo was growing increasingly anxious. Neither the raid on the bank in San José nor the stampede of Coulter cattle had achieved its objective of drawing any of them from the Two Bar X. He was amazed. Surely he could not have misjudged old Adam's character. Why hadn't he rounded up those sons of his, lashed them with his tongue, and sent them scouring the hills for whoever was disturbing the peace of his beloved ranch?

The band was becoming restless at the inactivity, even loyal Romero was heard to grumble, so Laredo decided to scout out the land himself.

Leaving the mountains once more, he crossed the badlands and approached the range in trepidation. Memories of Lucinda and the happy times they had spent were crowding in on him and he was filled with a great sadness.

Skirting the high ground overlooking the valley with its ribbon of clear water flowing through, he reined in suddenly, unable to believe his eyes. Ben Coulter, heading towards him. So he hadn't been killed in the stampede. He was crouched low in the saddle, looking neither to left or right, and riding as though all the devils in hell were after him.

Laredo's rifle was up in a flash and, taking careful aim, he fired. Ben threw up his arms and went hurtling off his mount. It reared, snorted and shot off along the valley.

Laredo manoeuvred his roan down the rocky hillside and rode up to view the body. Viciously he pumped more slugs into it, spat, and rode on. The hand which had wielded that rawhide whip was stilled forever.

With the sweet taste of revenge permeating his whole being, Laredo leisurely retraced his steps to the hide-out and Gomez in his look-out, seeing him from afar, waved his rifle in greeting. When Laredo eventually reached the burly bandit, he smiled down at him.

"All is well, amigo?"

Gomez shrugged despondently.

"Ah, senor — that gringo . . ."

Delaney again? Laredo suppressed a sigh.

"Never mind, Gomez. I have news for you. One of the Coulters is dead. Ben Coulter. Shot him clean out of his saddle. Now they will be coming for us but we'll be ready, eh amigo?"

"Senor!" breathed Gomez, his eyes suddenly alive.

"We must keep watch, more so than ever." Gomez patted his gun.

"Just let the gringos come, senor — I'll be waiting."

Laredo continued his upward climb and reaching the cavern saw that Delaney was squatting in the entrance, propped against the rock face and idly whittling a stick. He glanced up at Laredo's approach, noting with curiosity the look of satisfaction on his face. As usual he kept silent, as though it was beneath him to ask questions. It was a habit which greatly irritated Laredo. Only the fact that he was bursting with news forced him to speak out.

"Ben Coulter's dead," he said, getting down from his horse. "Caught him in a valley on the outskirts of town."

Delaney raised his eyebrows.

"Dead, huh? Sure this time?"

Snapped Laredo: "Of course I'm sure. Made certain of it."

"He was alone?"

"Yes — and in a hurry to reach town."

Delaney stroked his bristled chin. "One down and four to go, including Slim Jackson. Should have been three."

"Three? What do you mean, Delaney?"

"What I say, amigo — three. Saw Kit Coulter in town the other night and just missed him with my knife. Luckiest hombre this side of the Sierras."

"You never told me," Laredo said angrily.

"Why the hell should I? Missed him, didn't I?" Delaney carried on whittling.

"Good knife it was. Better than this damned thing."

Controlling his temper, Laredo said quietly. "The time has come for us to say adios, Delaney. I am in charge of this band and I want you to leave now. My amigos are not happy, senor. I shall pay you of course."

If he was taken aback by this sudden decision, Delaney didn't show it.

"Of course," he echoed, then added. "Suits me fine. One more day with these amigos is one too many." He stood up, threw away the stick and slid his knife back into the sheath. "I'm hauling ass, here and now. Where's the dinero?"

Laredo turned to the cave.

"Romero!"

Romero appeared in the entrance, smoking a cheroot.

"Senor?"

"Bring me the gold. Senor Delaney is leaving."

Romero looked, saw the expression on Laredo's face, and went inside without a word.

Laredo turned back to Delaney.

"You can take your share and mine also. I told you that I was not a *bandito*. You can also collect the money from that old scoundrel Sam Trenker. Maybe he has sold the horses by now. One more thing: we do not like each other Delaney, but I thank you for your help."

"Cut the cackle," sneered Delaney. "Just get the dinero — pronto."

By the time the gold was ready for him, Delaney had collected his blanket-roll, canteen and saddlebags, and was ready for the trail. In silence he checked his share, stuffed it into the bags and mounted. He moved off without a backward glance and the Mexicans watched until he was out of sight.

Romero was anxious.

"He will not betray us, senor?"

Laredo shook his head.

"No, my friend."

Delaney, he knew, wouldn't risk his hide by implicating himself with them.

Laredo was right of course. Delaney

had no intention of betraying the band and running the risk of implication, but their rejection of him when he was most needed rankled. Moreover his pride was hurt. Common sense told him to forget it but being Delaney he could not shake off this feeling of humiliation. How could he repay the Mexican without getting involved? He kept turning it over and over in his mind as he rode towards town until the whole matter grew out of proportion.

Greedy for every cent, he had every intention of calling on Indian Sam for the money for the posse's horses, but he knew that Trenker would not as yet have put through the deal so he decided to sleep overnight in Durward. The thought of a bed and a roof over his head after so many nights in the open warmed the cockles of his heart. No one knew him in town, so what the hell?

The 'Ace Saloon' was the nearest hotel, almost on the outskirts of town, and he booked a room. Having ensured the safety of his possessions, he lay down for a while, later joining one or two at the bar.

In the time it took to drink a couple of beers, he learned many things. First a bounty hunter called Forster had hit town and in a fancy display of shooting had foiled a raid on Stein's Bank. Five outlaws had been gunned down, four of whom were the notorious Galton brothers. The fifth was a guy with a scar. An hombre with the name of Mitchell. Next they talked of the Coulters and the killing of Ben, and it was only when someone spoke about the funeral to be held in town that Delaney's thoughts shot to Laredo.

A funeral in town. Surely, all the family would attend? That would mean the ranch being deserted except, no doubt, for Slim Jackson, the ranch foreman. Delaney's eyes gleamed. Laredo no *bandito?* He would make him appear to be the biggest bastard ever to tote a gun.

Delaney found Slim mending a fence.

He was all alone, but it didn't matter anyway. He would have enjoyed gunning down some greasers. Slim was at first suspicious of him but Delaney in his eloquent way soon allayed the foreman's fears and in a while they were sharing a drink. Slim told him all about the Coulters and the killing of Ben and how he'd like to get his hands on the goddam greaseball who'd started all this. Funeral? Naw — he hadn't attended. Someone gotta look after the range. Can't trust the peons. 'Sides, you couldn't get Slim Jackson to town. T'ain't safe. Not after the other night. Jest ridin' nice and peaceful with Mr Kit, then whizz. A knife, would you believe. From out of nowhere. Jest missed Mr Kit.

"Dangerous place, Durward," said Delaney solemnly.

"Dangerous? Yer darned tootin' it is, mister. Say — what did you say your name was?"

"Delaney. Heard of me?"

Slim shook his head. "N-no . . . cain't say I have. Heard tell of a gunslinger by

206

that name, but you — ."

The foreman couldn't finish the sentence, not with a knife sticking in his gut. In fact, he never spoke again; even when Delaney nailed him to the nearest tree. Just screams enough to petrify any living creature within earshot.

Delaney leisurely mounted and surveyed his handiwork. Let Laredo explain that away. Jackson was still shrieking as Delaney rode off across the range.

Part Four

17

Showdown at Durward

IN a clearing in the foothills of the Sierras three hundred braves and squaws of the Hopi sit in silence around a huge bonfire, the light playing capriciously on their paint-daubed faces.

The silence is broken by the beat of a single tom-tom, a slow rhythmic beat which grows quicker every minute.

Suddenly it stops and the faces turn towards a row of drummers beyond the fire. A dozen pairs of dusky hands are poised above the taut hides of the drums, then, down they come in unison, thunderously beating out the start of the Snake Dance. The volume increases, reverberating through the mountain passes. A coyote howls mournfully in protest and an eagle in its eyrie rolls a questioning eye.

Sitting cross-legged next to the Chief, resplendent in the full head-dress of the Hopi, Cade feels his pulse quicken as the first of the dancers leaps into the firelight with a wild, hysterical cry. The face is daubed diagonally with yellow and blue and his head-dress of eagle feathers bobs and sways to a rhythmic chant. On his bulging biceps are armlets of gold and in his hands a pair of flattened rattles. But all eyes are on his glistening torso for there writhe two multi-coloured rock-snakes with flat, trembling heads, open mouths and cotton-white fangs. Now he is joined by other dancers equally as colourful and even more wild, and all with snakes wrapped around them. The tempo of the drumbeats quickens and before the rivetted gaze of the onlookers the dancers leap and yell, now skilfully balancing on the balls of their feet, now throwing themselves headlong with terrifying shrieks. Then, as suddenly as it had begun, the dance ceases. The dancers remain still, allowing the snakes to slither from their glistening bodies and crawl unmolested towards the bush, messengers to the gods to bring rain. Cade, a longtime friend of the Hopi, had seen it all before.

In his search for Laredo and his band Cade knew that he could rely upon his Indian friends to supply him with as much information as they could although not helping him physically. The Hopi would have nothing to do with the white man's quarrels. Let them kill each other, the more the better. They wanted only to remain in peace in their mountain retreat, as their forefathers had done before them. Cade, however, they liked, and they were prepared to give him all the help they could short of braves. After all, had he not saved the lives of two of them from the soldiers in blue?

This Mexican and his band? No — they hadn't seen them. But if they were operating around Durward and San José, they were certain to be hiding out somewhere along the south-west trail, probably in the Dekker Pass. Cade agreed.

That was how he figured it and it was heartening to learn that the Hopi saw it the same way. The Dekker, eh? Some ride. Best leave the burro with the Indians, it would only hamper him. He was risking his life bringing in Laredo but, a man of deep pride himself, he sympathised with the young Mexican who had been sadistically beaten and humiliated beyond decency. And there were disturbing aspects about the whole affair which niggled him.

He was unloading the burro and handing out beads and trinkets to the braves when Sam Trenker rode up with three mounts in his train. Some of the braves went to meet him.

While admiring the horseflesh, Sam gave Cade a baleful, suspicious look.

"Get your scarface?"

"Uhuh."

"Showed up at my place a couple of days after you left. A mal hombre. Planted him, eh? Good."

"Still up to your games, eh Sam?"

Sam replied huffily:

"You collect boots an' saddles. Me, I collect horses."

Cade nodded at the ones he had brought in. "A nice haul. Where did you get them."

Sam looked pained.

"Shucks, Mr Forster . . . "

"Where did you get them, Sam?"

"Goddam it, man why you so plumb interested where I got 'em? What's it to you?"

"I know that stallion, Sam. Belongs to Ewan Butler, marshal at San Felipe. Now who brought it in?"

Sam began to whine.

"Mr Forster, you know I cain't . . . "

Cade knew Ewan Butler, liked him. Once they worked together, roping in a gunslinger called Red Bristow. Butler wouldn't have parted with that mount willingly. Cade felt his temper rising.

"Sam," he said, "If you don't tell me who brought in that stallion I'll take the hide off you."

Sam gulped and looked shiftily at the braves, now staring at him. He shook his head and swore. "Gunslinger by the name of Delaney. Him and half a dozen greasers."

Cade's eyes narrowed. "Greasers, you say?"

"Yup. Maybe not half a dozen. Three or four maybe . . . "

"One of them good-looking? Finger missing? Tallish?"

Sam rubbed his chin. "Yeah, come to think of it . . . There was one like that."

Cade let out a sigh.

"Sam, when are they coming to collect?"

"Not them, Mr Forster — only Delaney. Soon as I get back, I reckon."

"Right. Finish your deal with the Hopi, pronto. I'm riding back with you."

Alarmed, Sam squeaked: "I don't want no trouble Mr Forster. This Delaney's one chunk of goddam meanness and throws a mighty powerful gun . . . "

"Get your business over, Sam," snapped Cade.

While Sam sulkily collected payment for the horses Cade took his leave of the Hopi chief. He said little, but there was a wealth of meaning in his eyes as they shook hands, Indian fashion. Then Cade was in the saddle and looking across at Sam stuffing gold-dust into his saddlebags. "Get moving, sourdough," he said shortly. Sam scowled back at him. Cade turned to the Chief.

"*Vaya con Dios,*" he murmured, and the Chief replied also in Spanish, "*Hasta leugo, amigo.*"

Cade did not trust Indian Sam, and trekking towards his shack kept him where he could keep an eye on him — in front. Old he might be, but he was slippier than an eel. And he would favour Delaney before him: bounty hunters were too much on the side of the law.

Delaney.

Cade had heard of him but knew little about him. He operated outside Cade's normal territory. Was he now one of Laredo's outfit and knew where they were holed up? A long shot but worth trying.

It was growing dark when they reached the shack. It stood forlorn, dilapidated and shrouded in silence. Cade sheltered his horse then sat waiting in the lee of the shack. Sam busied himself indoors, fixing coffee and making up his bed.

Delaney showed up within the hour, still atingle from the gruesome killing of the ranch foreman. From the shadows of the shack, Cade watched him dismount. "Freeze," he said crisply.

Delaney stopped dead, hand on the pommel of his saddle.

"Name's Forster — Cade Forster. I want information, and I want it quick. Where's Laredo holed up?"

Forster, thought Delaney — bounty hunter who had shot down Mitch and the Galtons. But where did he tie in with Laredo? The Coulters must have hired him. Why not tell him where Laredo was hiding out? Goddam greaser wanted cutting down to size.

Peering into the gloom, Delaney answered, "Dekker Pass, cave near the top. Got another four greasers with him.

Sam tell you I was with him?"

"Sort of. And now you've quit?"

"Yep. Folk in Durward are still talking about you, Forster; how you gunned down Mitch and the Galtons. Now you aiming to collect Laredo's scalp?"

"My business, Delaney."

"Yeh, and this is my business. Sam!"

The old man teetered in the doorway in an agony of apprehension. The tension between the two could almost be felt. Their words hung in the night air.

"Y-yes . . . " he quavered.

"Deal go through?"

"Sure it did. Got the dinero ready for you."

Delaney made towards the door and Cade stood up. "Freeze, I said."

Delaney stood still.

"Knew a marshal once who was mighty proud of his horse. Certain-sure he wouldn't have let some cheap gunslinger like you, Delaney, have it. When did you gun down Ewan Butler?"

Cade moved into the open, his eyes flint hard.

Delaney went pale and ran his tongue around his dry lips. There was no escaping this bounty killer.

"Delaney," said Cade quietly, "I'll give you the chance you've denied to others. But I warn you: no gunslinger ever shaded Cade Forster. Draw, you bastard!"

The execution was swift and deadly. Before Delaney's guns were out of their holsters Cade's were blasting orange flame, spinning him round until he collapsed into a bloodied heap on the hard, stony ground.

Cade blew away smoke from his shooting-irons and returned them to their holsters. He waited until Delaney had stopped twitching then turned to an open-mouthed Sam. "I'll have that coffee now."

Romero stirred, sat up and reached for a smoke. The cavern was silent but for the rumbling of Gomez, asleep at his side. He lit the cheroot and glanced at Laredo propping himself against the rock face.

In the flickering light of the torch his face looked tired and drawn.

Romero's heart went out to him. Laredo was no *bandito* and this way of life was foreign to him. But for those arrogant gringos he wouldn't be living it. Why had they tied him to a buckboard and flayed him so savagely? He hadn't confided in him and he hadn't asked, but he shared his hatred of them. Romero had watched him brood for hours on end. Sometimes he would leave the band, never said where he was going, but always returned. No explanation, just an aggravating silence. Still, the band remained loyal to him, each of them owing a debt he could not repay. Romero saved from a hanging and the other three from life-imprisonment. If only he could be persuaded to give up this vendetta they would gladly take their share of the San José robbery and make for the border.

"Laredo . . ."

The cry, low and controlled, shattered the silence and went re-echoing along the mountain pass.

Laredo and Romero jumped to their feed, exchanging looks. Gomez shook his head and sat up. *"Quien es?"*

There was a shot, then another, and Laredo was outside with Romero at his side. It was pitch-dark and rain was falling lightly.

"Pedro, Tomas — hold your fire," ordered Laredo. Now Gomez was at his side, clutching his rifle and peering into the darkness.

"Quit firing, Laredo — I'm alone."

Laredo drew himself up. "You are a brave man, Senor Forster," he called into the night. The bandits at his side looked at him in surprise.

"And you are a foolish one," came the voice from the darkness. "Call off your men. It's time we parleyed."

Laredo hesitated and Romero gripped his arm. "A trick, amigo."

"No, Romero — one against five? I think not." Laredo raised his voice.

"Let him through, amigos."

Cade swept off his hat, knocked off the rain and turned to face Laredo. "Cade Forster, senor — but then you already know. Works fast, our friend. Mind if I take the weight off my feet? Plumb tuckered out scaling these heights."

Laredo nodded and Cade squatted on Gomez' pile of blankets. The Mexican looked down on him and liked what he saw. In spite of himself he could feel suspicion subside.

"As I say you are a brave man — putting yourself in the lion's den."

"And as I say, Laredo, you are a foolish one." Cade glanced at the band. They were huddled in the mouth of the cavern, out of earshot. "Why do you keep on working for him?"

"Why not, senor? Freed me from a stake-out, didn't he? And he hates Adam Coulter as much as I do. How much do you know of this affair, Senor Forster?"

"Call me Cade, even my enemies do. How much do I know? Everything. Maria told me most, and . . ."

"Maria!" snarled Laredo. "That bitch who betrayed us . . . "

"Maria never betrayed you, you dumbhead. If she had, she would be taking it easy at the Two Bar X instead of whoring herself in the 'Silver Dollar' to scratch a living. Use your sense, Laredo. God, he's sure taken you for a ride. What's he told you? That Maria betrayed you to get in cahoots with the family? What a horse-laugh." Cade lowered his voice, watching the conflict of emotions on the other's face. "Can't you see it all, amigo? He frees you from the stake-out and in gratitude you go gunning down first Ben, then you hope, Adam, and he inherits the ranch. All nice and dandy. He pays you off handsomely and you vamoose over the border. Tipped you off when Coulter gold was in the San José bank and where and when the cattle drive was taking place. Figured he could afford to lose some of the dinero with such high stakes as the Two Bar X. Had it all weighed up, hadn't he? He knew damn fine you'd go gunning for Adam and Ben once you were freed from the stake-out but ask yourself, Laredo . . . how were you caught in the first place? Because Kit Coulter made goddam sure you were."

Laredo was stunned, couldn't take his eyes off Cade looking up at him earnestly.

He remained silent for several moments, then his lips began to move. Cade could just hear what he was saying. "But if Maria did not tell, how did . . . "

"Kit Coulter knew you were seeing her?" murmured Cade. "Wondered how long it would take before you got round to it."

18

ADAM COULTER sat bolt upright in his high-backed chair staring intently at the two riders slowly approaching the ranch-house. The sun was riding high, shedding a golden light over the rain-sodden grass. As they drew nearer, he recognised one of them — Cade Forster, the bounty hunter. The other he didn't know. Only that he was a Mexican judging by his wide-brimmed sombrero and tapaderos.

"Martha!" he bawled.

She appeared in the doorway, wiping her hands on her apron.

"What is it?"

He was pointing at the window, his face and gesture agitated. "Ain't that Forster, the hire gun?"

Martha looked out.

"Yes," she said in wonder. "But who's that with him?"

"Just what I want to know, woman. Go and find out . . . No wait. What in hell . . . " He stopped short, his thin mouth an inverted crescent. Lucinda, darting from the house and across the patio towards the pair. He heard her cries: "Juan, Juan . . . "

The Mexican had dismounted, waiting for her. The bounty hunter sat astride his bay, watching impassively. Now she was in the Mexican's arms and burying her head in his chest but he stood quite still gazing at her ash-blonde hair. Her head went up and she saw his face. It was as hard as marble. "Juan — " she faltered.

Their eyes met but only for one brief moment, then she felt a sharp stab of pain between her shoulder-blades. "Juan!" she gasped. Her brain began to swim and she felt weak at the knees. Her eyes began to glaze over and she felt herself falling, falling . . .

Gently he lowered her to the ground and as she rolled to one side the hilt of the knife was clearly visible, sticking from her back. Laredo watched in silence as blood began to trickle from her mouth staining the patio. Martha, unable to believe her eyes, stood horrified in the doorway. She was speechless. Certain that Lucinda was dead, Laredo crossed himself and looked up at Cade. "It is done, senor."

Cade replied tersely: "Yes. Now get to hell out of here."

Laredo gave him a lingering, hostile look then swung round his horse's head and galloped off towards the plain.

Cade got down from his mount, gathered Lucinda in his arms and withdrew the blade. Wiping it clean, he stuck the knife into his belt and stood up with her.

Martha stood back and pointed to a door inside. "Put — put her in there." She caught her breath, then, "What kind of man are you to let it happen?"

"Don't waste pity on her, Mrs Coulter. She had it coming."

Cade pushed open the door with his foot and laid the body on a couch, then taking his sweat-rag wiped clean her mouth. Over his shoulder he asked, "Where is the old bastard? Same room as before?"

"Y-yes . . . But don't hurt him. He's old — "

Cade said grimly: "Ma'am, I don't aim to hurt Adam Coulter. There's nothing that I could do or say that would hurt him more than he's done himself." His tone softened. "Come and hear for yourself."

Adam cringed in his chair, his face both livid and fearful. Cade knew that he had seen all through the window. He said quietly: "Don't waste pity on her, Mr Coulter. If she had had her way you would have been lying on that couch in there, not her. When I came to this ranch you told me that Laredo raped your daughter but you were wrong. Sure, you thought so, you all did, because she said she had been, but Laredo didn't attack your daughter. She told you that so you would have him flogged then staked-out, like you always do to anyone who crosses you.

A guy like you wouldn't have let off a greaser with just a flogging. There had to be something more and Maria, her servant, told me what you had done. You can relax, Mr Coulter. I am not going to hurt you."

Cade paused, giving time for his words to sink in and for Adam, unnerved by the killing of Lucinda, to get control of himself. Fear was slowly subsiding in his thin face giving way, to hatred and loathing. "Lies," he snarled. "Lies . . . "

Cade straddled a chair, facing him.

"No, Mr Coulter — pin back your ears and listen . . . "

"Lies. You bring that greaseball here to my ranch, a bandit who has killed my son, crucified my foreman and now stabbed my daughter in front of my own eyes . . . Martha, where in hell's Kit? Where's Jess?" He thumped his stick in blind fury.

Martha sprang to her feet and rushed to his side. "Calm yourself, calm yourself. More of this and you'll take a stroke." She flashed a look of hate at Cade, lighting a smoke. "I think you've said enough. You'd better leave."

"Not until you've heard everything, then I'll be glad to haul my ass out of this goddam place. Maria told me a whole heap more than the stake-out. How for weeks Laredo was meeting *his* daughter down by the river until she persuaded him to come into the house . . . "

"*Lies!*" yelled Adam for the fourth time. "She wouldn't have dared. A greaser under my roof?"

"Three times, helped by Maria, and on the third occasion he was caught and she cried, 'rape'. She'd grown tired of Laredo and saw a way of getting rid of him and she had bigger things on her mind — the ranch itself. Ask yourselves — who went back to the badlands that night to free Laredo from the stake-out. Not Lucinda. She wouldn't have known where he was and in any case would have been too scared. It was Kit of course. They were in cahoots to get rid of you, Mr Coulter, then Ben, and inherit the ranch. And Laredo, burning for revenge, was going

231

to do it for them. Poor sap was grateful to Kit for having saved his life, never realising that he and Lucinda had set the whole thing up. Kit told Laredo about the money in the San Jose bank and the cattle drive. Reckoned he could afford to lose some of the dinero he would inherit. Well, Mr Coulter, like I said you built up a good spread, too good it seems for some of your family. They couldn't wait to get their hands on it. Maybe if you had given more of your time to them instead of the ranch all this might never have happened. Still, maybe not. After all, they're Coulters."

Cade got to his feet and doused his smoke. He glanced at Adam slumped in his chair, defeated. He said quietly: "Laredo got the last laugh even though he'll carry those scars with him to the grave.

He made for the door and turned, compassion in his look. It hadn't been easy shattering two people's worlds, telling one that his son and daughter had plotted to have him killed and the other that her brother-in-law had been instrumental in the shooting down of her husband.

Martha sat stunned, then murmured something which at first puzzled Cade.

"They were close, too close . . . "

Kit and Lucinda.

Handsome brother and too lovely a sister.

What part had jealousy played in breaking up her affair with Laredo?

Cade stepped into the sunlight and shaking off the gloom crossed to where his horse stood patiently tethered. He felt bone-weary, and not only from his night in the mountains.

19

CROUCHED along the ridge the bandits grimly waited with their rifles trained on the horseman in the draw below, the place where their leader had been conducting his clandestine meetings over the past few weeks. They couldn't hear what the two were saying to each other but waited patiently for the signal to fire.

Laredo was astride a mustang and Kit Coulter, blissfully unaware of his danger, his chestnut. The sun hung in the sky like a ball of fire. The Mexican tightened his grip on the reins with one hand and held up the other. Romero was the first to fire, followed rapidly by Gomez, Pedro and Tomas.

Startled, Kit's horse reared, throwing his slug-ridden body into the dust, and bolted out of the draw. Calmly drawing his belt guns, Laredo emptied the contents of both into the twitching corpse.

Romero stood up, brandishing his rifle.

"All is well, amigo?"

Laredo leaned forward and patted his mustang's neck.

"All is well, Romero."

It was quiet and peaceful along the river bank and Cade slept in the shade of the trees until evening closed in. Refreshed, he rode into Durward, and passing Jake La Rue's establishment, heard a voice above the clamour which he recognised — Emma Carson's.

"What if you are having his kid, Nell? Maybe a son to take care of you in your old age. Just think — another Jess Coulter."

"Coulter be damned," said another girl. "Jess James — after me."

"Don't sound right, Nell."

"Okay — Jesse James."

Cade rode on and dismounted at the 'Silver Dollar'. The saloon was in full swing. Ignoring the dubious antics of

Arkansas Amy and her troupe he went up to the bar. "Shot of rye, Charlie."

The bar-keep looked round in surprise.

"Mr Forster! Sure glad to see you back." He poured a drink and pushed it over to Cade. "Things have been happening since you left town. Slim Jackson, foreman at the Two Bar X, found with a knife in his gut and nailed to a tree. Folk reckon it's Apache work. God help us if them varmints are on the loose again. Means a job for the pony-soldiers."

Jackson — nailed to a tree. Even Laredo in his burning hatred wouldn't have done that, thought Cade. More like Delaney.

"Town gets worse," grumbled Charlie. "Couple of guys were clubbed to death last night just outside the saloon and three gunned down in the 'Western Star'. This burg wants a marshal, no cheap tin-horn but the real McCoy. Someone like Ulysses Rowntree up Mesa way."

Cade tossed back his drink.

"Room still vacant?"

Charlie grinned.

"Sure is, and smelling worse than Simpson's funeral parlour. Maria. Flowers every day since you left. Certain she was that you'd show up again. Talks of no one else but you, Mr Forster. Shame she has to work here. Nobody knows why she quit the Two Bar X."

Cade had another shot of rye then made his way upstairs. The room was as neat and tidy as ever but with a difference, flowers were everywhere, filling the air with their fragrance.

Cade tossed his hat on the bed, unbuckled his holster-belt and slung it over the back of a chair. The din from below was growing worse. He went to the window and stood gazing at the bank opposite. It seemed ages ago since he had shot down scar-faced Joe Mitchell and the Galton brothers. The door burst open and he swung round. Maria, wide-eyed and so excited she could hardly speak. "Senor!"

"Come in, Maria." His eyes went round the room. "Sure smells nice in here."

She flushed. "I-I've prayed for you every hour . . ."

Cade nodded and smiled at her.

"Come and sit down. There's a lot you should know."

"Did you find Juan?"

"Yeh — I found him all right."

"Where is he now?"

"Half way to the border, if he's any sense. Sit down, gal."

Maria crossed to a chair and sat gazing up at him.

"I don't know how well you knew Lucinda Coulter but I can tell you that she was meaner than a rattler . . ."

"Miss Lucinda?" gasped Maria.

"Shortly after meeting Laredo she saw a way of getting rid of old Adam and Ben and taking over the ranch. She was in cahoots with her twin brother Kit. She sweet-talked Laredo into visiting her in the house and then cried 'rape'. He was flogged and staked-out, Kit freed him and the poor dupe out of gratitude and seeking revenge did their work for them. First Ben was killed then it would have been Adam's turn. Jess didn't matter. They would have inherited the spread. Comes as a shock to you, eh gal?"

Maria shook her head in wonder. "Miss Lucinda . . . I-I cannot believe it . . . "

"Yeh — looked as though butter wouldn't melt in her mouth. But she was mean all right. Only two people knew that his name was Laredo, Lucinda and you, so how did the others know who he was — a guy they'd never seen. You wouldn't tell so it must have been Lucinda. Who had she told, and why? She'd taken someone into her confidence and I figured it was Kit. When Ben was shot down, I knew it was Kit. She fooled you, Maria, like she did the rest. Set the whole thing up. Got Laredo into the house three times and on the third time Kit was waiting. He got hold of Ben and Jess and I guess you know the rest. The family genuinely thought that Laredo had attacked and raped her."

"Juan?"

"Blamed you for everything. Kit told Laredo that you had informed on him and Lucinda — "

"Me?"

"Yes — to get into cahoots with Adam and the family. He didn't know that they'd slung you out until I told him. Then it dawned on him that it could only have been Lucinda herself. He's taken his revenge, Maria. Came back with me to the Two Bar X and killed her. Knifed her in the back. She's gone and so is Ben. Adam's a broken old man so he's got his revenge."

"But — "

"Kit Coulter? He's got it coming, I guess. From the time he freed Laredo from the stake-out they have been meeting in a draw out in the foothills and somehow I think this'll be the last time. Like I say, he's probably crow-bait by now and Laredo halfway to the border. Well gal, reckon we've talked enough about the Coulters. Service in this saloon still as good as ever?"

"Service?"

"Yeh — the service. Still as good as ever?"

Maria's mind, already in a whirl, failed to grasp his implication at first, then her eyes went even wider. "B-but senor . . . You said 'never' . . . "

Cade grinned sheepishly and pulled at his nose. "Well," he said slowly, "I reckon even Cade Forster can change his mind. Time I hung up my shooting-irons anyway, and know something, gal? There's a small spread near San Ferento — "

Cade didn't finish what he was saying. Maria had sprung from the chair, flung her arms around him and standing on tip-toe waited eagerly. He brought his mouth down on hers and thrilled to the touch of her full, soft lips. Her mouth was like a rosebud with the dew still on it.

Other titles in the
Linford Western Library:

TOP HAND
Wade Everett

The Broken T was big. But no ranch is big enough to let a man hide from himself.

GUN WOLVES OF LOBO BASIN
Lee Floren

The Feud was a blood debt. When Smoke Talbot found the outlaws who gunned down his folks he aimed to nail their hide to the barn door.

SHOTGUN SHARKEY
Marshall Grover

The westbound coach carrying the indomitable Larry and Stretch headed for a shooting showdown.

BRETT RANDALL, GAMBLER
E. B. Mann

Larry Day had the choice of running away from the law or of assuming a dead man's place. No matter what he decided he was bound to end up dead.

THE GUNSHARP
William R. Cox

The Eggerleys weren't very smart. They trained their sights on Will Carney and Arizona's biggest blood bath began.

THE DEPUTY OF SAN RIANO
Lawrence A. Keating and
Al. P. Nelson

When a man fell dead from his horse, Ed Grant was spotted riding away from the scene. The deputy sheriff rode out after him and came up against everything from gunfire to dynamite.

HELL RIDERS
Steve Mensing

Wade Walker's kid brother, Duane, was locked up in the Silver City jail facing a rope at dawn. Wade was a ruthless outlaw, but he was smart, and he had vowed to have his brother out of jail before morning!

DESERT OF THE DAMNED
Nelson Nye

The law was after him for the murder of a marshal — a murder he didn't commit. Breen was after him for revenge — and Breen wouldn't stop at anything . . . blackmail, a frameup . . . or murder.

DAY OF THE COMANCHEROS
Steven C. Lawrence

Their very name struck terror into men's hearts — the Comancheros, a savage army of cutthroats who swept across Texas, leaving behind a blood-stained trail of robbery and murder.

SUNDANCE: SILENT ENEMY
John Benteen

A lone crazed Cheyenne was on a personal war path. They needed to pit one man against one crazed Indian. That man was Sundance.

LASSITER
Jack Slade

Lassiter wasn't the kind of man to listen to reason. Cross him once and he'll hold a grudge for years to come — if he let you live that long.

LAST STAGE TO GOMORRAH
Barry Cord

Jeff Carter, tough ex-riverboat gambler, now had himself a horse ranch that kept him free from gunfights and card games. Until Sturvesant of Wells Fargo showed up.

GUNSLINGER'S RANGE
Jackson Cole

Three escaped convicts are out for revenge. They won't rest until they put a bullet through the head of the dirty snake who locked them behind bars.

RUSTLER'S TRAIL
Lee Floren

Jim Carlin knew he would have to stand up and fight because he had staked his claim right in the middle of Big Ike Outland's best grass.

THE TRUTH ABOUT SNAKE RIDGE
Marshall Grover

The troubleshooters came to San Cristobal to help the needy. For Larry and Stretch the turmoil began with a brawl and then an ambush.

DONOVAN
Elmer Kelton

Donovan was supposed to be dead. Uncle Joe Vickers had fired off both barrels of a shotgun into the vicious outlaw's face as he was escaping from jail. Now Uncle Joe had been shot — in just the same way.

CODE OF THE GUN
Gordon D. Shirreffs

MacLean came riding home, with saddle tramp written all over him, but sewn in his shirt-lining was an Arizona Ranger's star.

GAMBLER'S GUN LUCK
Brett Austen

Gamblers seldom live long. Parker was a hell of a gambler. It was his life — or his death . . .

ORPHAN'S PREFERRED
Jim Miller

Sean Callahan answers the call of the Pony Express and fights Indians and outlaws to get the mail through.

DAY OF THE BUZZARD
T. V. Olsen

All Val Penmark cared about was getting the men who killed his wife.

THE MANHUNTER
Gordon D. Shirreffs

Lee Kershaw knew that every Rurale in the territory was on the lookout for him. But the offer of $5,000 in gold to find five small pieces of leather was too good to turn down.